Acting Edition

Just Like Us

by Karen Zacarías

Based on the Book by
Helen Thorpe

SAMUEL FRENCH

No one shall make any changes in this title(s) for the purpose of production. No part of this book may be reproduced, stored in a retrieval system, scanned, uploaded, or transmitted in any form, by any means, now known or yet to be invented, including mechanical, electronic, digital, photocopying, recording, videotaping, or otherwise, without the prior written permission of the publisher. No one shall share this title(s), or any part of this title(s), through any social media or file hosting websites.

For all inquiries regarding motion picture, television, online/digital and other media rights, please contact Concord Theatricals Corp.

MUSIC AND THIRD-PARTY MATERIALS USE NOTE

Licensees are solely responsible for obtaining formal written permission from copyright owners to use copyrighted music and/or other copyrighted third-party materials (e.g. artworks, logos) in the performance of this play and are strongly cautioned to do so. If no such permission is obtained by the licensee, then the licensee must use only original music and materials that the licensee owns and controls. Licensees are solely responsible and liable for clearances of all third-party copyrighted materials, including without limitation music, and shall indemnify the copyright owners of the play(s) and their licensing agent, Concord Theatricals Corp., against any costs, expenses, losses and liabilities arising from the use of such copyrighted third-party materials by licensees. For music, please contact the appropriate music licensing authority in your territory for the rights to any incidental music.

IMPORTANT BILLING AND CREDIT REQUIREMENTS

If you have obtained performance rights to this title, please refer to your licensing agreement for important billing and credit requirements.

JUST LIKE US was first produced by The Denver Center (Kent Thompson, Producing Artistic Director) at The Stage Theatre on October 4, 2013. The performance was directed by Kent Thompson. The assistant director was José Antonio Mercado. The set designer was Kevin Regdon, and the costume designer was Kevin Copenhaver. The lighting designer was Don Darnutzer and the projection designer was Charlie I. Miller. The sound designer was Craig Breitenbach, and the composer was Deborah Wicks La Puma. The movement coach was Laurence Curry and the dramaturg was Douglas Langworthy. The voice and dialect coach was Kathryn G. Maes PhD and the Spanish coach was Gabriella Cavallero. The cast was as follows:

HELEN THORPE	Mary Bacon
MARISELA/RAÚL GÓMEZ GARCÍA	Yunuen Pardo
YADIRA/SPANISH TRANSLATOR	Adriana Gaviria
CLARA	Cynthia Bastidas
ELISSA/ZULEMA/SANDRA RIVAS	Ruth Livier
FABIÁN/TOM TANCREDO/ENSEMBLE	Richard Azurdia
JOSEFA/ALMA/DONNIE'S MOTHER	Alma Martinez
YOLANDA/CYNTHIA POUNDSTONE	Gabriella Cavallero
JULIO/RAMIRO/ENSEMBLE	Fidel Gomez
RECRUITER/MIKE McGARRY/ENSEMBLE	Steven Cole Hughes
MR. SMITH/JIM SPENCE/ENSEMBLE	Cajardo Rameer Lindsey
CARLOS/CÉZAR MESQUITA/ENSEMBLE	Felix Solis
IRENE CHÁVEZ/ANA/ENSEMBLE	Liza Fernandez
LUKE/BAILIFF/ENSEMBLE	Casey Predovic

CHARACTERS

PRINCIPALS

HELEN THORPE – Forties. The reporter. Irish American Quaker, very smart, confident, unfussy, woman with a penchant for interesting eyeglasses. Highly-educated career woman married to the Mayor of Denver. Mother of one small child. Much more comfortable as a thoughtful observer than as the center of attention. Prefers being a reporter than First Lady of Denver. Strongly convicted in her principles, she is self-aware about her role, and is consistently fair-minded.

MARISELA – Eighteen to twenty-two. Fully bilingual and bicultural Mexican. Does not have legal papers to be in the country. Emotional, sassy, intelligent, energetic, ambitious, yet sometimes insecure, a bundle of contradictions, attracted to bad boys yet is a great student. She craves excitement, wears a lot of makeup, tight jeans, and loves loud music (Ranchera especially).

YADIRA – Eighteen to twenty-two. Fully bilingual, bicultural Mexican. Does not have legal papers to be in the country. Still waters run deep. Beautiful, reserved, smart young woman who craves stability and security. Marisela's best friend, yet polar opposite in manner and look. Wears skinny jeans and bare-midriff shirts and yet, isn't a party girl at all.

CLARA – Eighteen to twenty-two. Bilingual, bicultural Mexican. In the U.S. legally. Innocent, religious, earnest girl. Good student. Hard worker. Discreet clothes, no makeup, wears a cross every day. The peacemaker and dreamer.

ELISSA – Eighteen to twenty-two. Bilingual and bicultural. In the U.S. legally. The go-getter, team captain of the group. Good student. Hard worker.

FABIÁN – Thirties to forties. Marisela's hard working, sometimes grouchy father. Only Spanish-speaking. A janitor at a supermarket who loves his family and worries about Marisela's wild ways. In the U.S. without legal status.

JOSEFA – Thirties to forties. Marisela's Mexican mother. Spanish-speaking. A devoted mother and hard working cleaning lady who looks after her four kids in the U.S.

YOLANDA – Twenties. Brassy bilingual hairdresser.

JULIO – Twenties, Latino.

SUPPORTING AND ENSEMBLE ROLES

TOM TANCREDO – A second generation Italian-American Congressman born in a working-class neighborhood in Denver who now represents a very affluent neighborhood in Colorado. The leading voice in Congress against illegal immigration. Charismatic, smart, loud, affable, and very single-minded in his fervor against illegal immigration. Can be doubled by **FABIÁN**.

RECRUITER – Named Tom Johnson. Can be doubled by **FABIÁN**.

CARLOS – Yadira's stepfather. Can be doubled by **FABIÁN**.

CÉZAR MESQUITA – Can be doubled by **FABIÁN**.

FEDERICO PEÑA – Can be doubled by **FABIÁN**.

COP – Can be doubled by **FABIÁN**.

RAÚL GOMÉZ GARCÍA – Is doubled by **MARISELA**.

ZULEMA – Yadira's younger sister. Can be doubled by **ELISSA**.

MRS. SMITH – Can be doubled by **JOSEFA**.

CAROL VIZZI – Can be doubled by **JOSEFA**.

LISA MARTÍNEZ – Can be doubled by **JOSEFA** or **YOLANDA**.

ANA – Can be doubled by **YOLANDA**.

CYNTHIA POUNDSTONE – Can be doubled by **YOLANDA**.

LUCY – Can be doubled by **YOLANDA**.

LOCAL BUSINESS LADY – Can be doubled by **YOLANDA**.

RAMIRO – Can be doubled by **JULIO**.

MIKE McGARRY – Can be doubled by **JULIO**.

Licensees can cast according to their cast size. Additional **ENSEMBLE** roles can be assigned from the Supporting and Ensemble characters.

ACT ONE

Scene: Marisela's Bedroom

(Lively Ranchera music.)*

(Projection: Pictures of Denver. Welcome to Denver sign. Images of the airport, the Convention Center, the Theater, the streets, the Rockies, affluent neighborhood, streets, and then the neighborhood where Marisela lives.)*

*(****HELEN**** walks on to the stage. She looks at the audience.)*

HELEN. Tonight is a very special night in the lives of four best friends I recently met.

And it is a special day for me, because I get to be a small part of it.

*(****MARISELA, YADIRA, CLARA,**** and ****ELISSA**** in fabulous prom dresses enter dancing along to the Ranchera song.)*

---

* A license to produce *Just Like Us* does not include a performance license for any third-party or copyrighted music, or a license to publicly display any third-party or copyrighted images. Licensees should create an original composition or use music in the public domain. Licensees must also acquire rights for any copyrighted images or create their own. For further information, please see the Music and Third-Party Materials Use Note on page iii.

(They stop dancing and start getting ready for prom.)

*(**FABIÁN** and **JOSEFA**, Marisela's parents, come in.)*

FABIÁN. ¡Marisela, voy a ir contigo!

MARISELA. ¡Mami, dile a Papi, que no puede venir conmigo!

JOSEFA. ¡Ay, pues no sé qué decir!

FABIÁN. ¡Yo soy tu padre!

MARISELA. ¡Mami, habla con él!

JOSEFA. ¡Fabián!

FABIÁN. ¡Josefa, es que no me gusta!

*(**FABIÁN** storms off and exits.)*

*(**JOSEFA** follows him and exits.)*

ELISSA, YADIRA & CLARA. Uy, Marisela.

MARISELA. My Papi says he's coming to prom!

ELISSA. Marisela, nobody goes to prom with a chaperone.

CLARA. He's just worried about the boys.

YADIRA. Clara, he's worried about Fernando.

ELISA. But Fernando is working in Arizona.

MARISELA. It's a secret, but Fernando is driving from Arizona to be here tonight with me at the prom.

ELISSA. Driving a thousand miles in one day?

MARISELA. I haven't seen him in six months.

CLARA. That's so romantic. Like Romeo and Juliet.

YADIRA. Except Romeo's horse is an old truck.

ELISSA. It's crazy. Fernando is too old for you. And your Papi is bound to find out!

HELEN. Elissa: The bossy one. If the four girls had been a sports team, Elissa would be their captain.

MARISELA. Clara, I have to see Fernando. You have to cover for me.

CLARA. Ay, Marisela…no sé…

HELEN. Clara: The sensitive one. Sweet. No makeup. No boyfriend. Parents believe her with good reason.

MARISELA. Besides, it's not cool for a father to go to prom.

YADIRA. Cool is not the best argument for your Papi.

HELEN. Yadira: The poised one: organized, serious, and very private.

MARISELA. Please, guys! You have to help me! Prom is the most important night of our lives!!!

HELEN. Marisela: the dramatic one: Emotional. Loud. A straight-A student who also likes to party.

CLARA. Oye Marisela, your dress still has a price tag – oh my God. That's like a month of work for you.

MARISELA. It's still Ross Dress for Less.

YADIRA. Not less enough for me.

MARISELA. I couldn't help myself. I'm an elegant woman. And this is prom.

ELISSA. And then we get to dress for up for graduation.

YADIRA. Graduation. I can't wait. I just can't stand being around my stepdad anymore.

MARISELA. Ugh. Maybe your Mom will leave him.

YADIRA. No, I think she's stuck.

MARISELA. Don't talk about sad things Yadira. It's making your hair limp.

ELISSA. I thought you got Yolanda to come and do our hair.

      (**MARISELA** *sprays* **YADIRA**'s *hair. It's huge.*)

YADIRA. Oh God!

MARISELA. That's great!

ELISSA. Hand me the hairspray.

MARISELA. Do you want me to do your makeup, Clara?

CLARA. You can do my nails.

MARISELA. What? You don't like how I do my makeup?

CLARA. I'm already wearing too much makeup!

MARISELA. It's too simple.

ELISSA. Let Clara be Clara!

      (**YOLANDA,** *big hair and colorful clothes, bursts in with makeup and hair stuff.*)

YOLANDA. Hola, nenas!

GIRLS. *(Annoyed.)* YOLANDA!

YOLANDA. ¡Aquí estoy! To make you beautiful for el prom.

CLARA. ¡Gracias a Dios!

YOLANDA. *(To* **MARISELA.***)* I just talked to your Papi. He's a mess.

MARISELA. Mi Papi is worried because he doesn't understand prom.

YOLANDA. He is worried because he understands boys. Who's up first?

ALL. Marisela.

YOLANDA. ¡Órale! You girls are going to look requete chulas!

GIRLS. Gracias.

YOLANDA. Prom! Graduation!

MARISELA. It's all happening so fast.

YOLANDA. *(To* **MARISELA.***)* So what are you going to do after graduation? Are you going to get another job? Are you and Fernando going to get married?

MARISELA. No. I'm going to college!

YOLANDA. Going to college? Really? Where?

(Pause. A change in the mood.)

MARISELA. I don't know. Nowhere yet. I'm waiting to hear.

YOLANDA. You girls waiting too?

ALL GIRLS. *(Subdued.)* Yes.

YOLANDA. College! Válgame Dios. You girls must be so smart. And so rich! You are going to el college?!!!

MARISELA. Trying…trying…trying.

YOLANDA. Is that why there's a white lady sitting in the corner, taking notes?

*(***ALL** *turn to look at* **HELEN.** **HELEN** *looks up.)*

HELEN. Oh. Hello.

YADIRA. Oh. That's Helen.

CLARA. Helen Thorpe.

MARISELA. She's married to John Hickenlooper, the mayor of Denver!

ELISSA. Helen is the First Lady of Denver!!!

CLARA. I love how fancy that sounds.

HELEN. I feel a little miscast in that role. *(Goes to introduce herself.)* Hello, Yolanda, nice to meet you.

YOLANDA. If you're the mayor's wife then what are you doing here?

HELEN. I'm a reporter.

YOLANDA. Ay no! A reporter!

CLARA. A very respected journalist –

YADIRA. – and she's is writing an article in a magazine.

MARISELA. About us!!!!

YOLANDA. What did you girls do wrong?

GIRLS. NOTHING!

YOLANDA. Valgame! There has to be something! Reporters always want bad news.

HELEN. A fair reporter wants news: good and bad.

YOLANDA. And you, First Lady Helen, you are...fair?

HELEN. I hope so. I strive to be. That's why I am here. That's why I am listening.

MARISELA. You hear that, Yolanda, Helen is listening. To us.

ELISSA. She's on our side.

HELEN. I'm not on any side. I'm here to learn.

YOLANDA. Interesting. So Helen, hablas español?

HELEN. Un poco. Quiero aprender más.

> *(A cluck of appreciation by all the girls for her Spanish and her interest.)*

MARISELA. Nice job, Helen.

HELEN. I hope I will learn more in the process of writing the article.

YOLANDA. Ah *(Beat.)* An article about you? Is that safe?

ELISSA. Of course it's...safe.

YOLANDA. For you, maybe, Elissa. But is it safe for all of you? I don't think so.

(They all look at **HELEN.***)*

HELEN. I won't use your real names. I'll change the name of your high school. Protecting a source is part of a journalist's ethic.

MARISELA. See? Helen is going to protect us.

YOLANDA. I hope so. Because if the wrong people find you, you and your parents will lose everything.

(A car honks.)

MARISELA. The boys are here!

(The **GIRLS** *scramble to get ready.)*

¡Ay! Hairspray!

(The **GIRLS** *line up and* **YOLANDA** *covers the girls' hair with hairspray.)*

YOLANDA. Wait! We need a photo! Foto.

HELEN. We can use my camera!

(The **FOUR GIRLS** *pose.)*

One, two, three.

GIRLS. ¡Queso!

(A flash.)

(Another car honk. The **GIRLS** *shriek!)*

ELISSA. We gotta go!

YOLANDA. Have fun!

MARISELA. We will!

YOLANDA. But not too much fun!

YADIRA. OK ladies…prom officially begins.

ELISSA. Right…

CLARA. Now.

ALL. ¡Órale!

> (*As the* **GIRLS** *exit.*)

HELEN. Elissa was born a U.S. citizen.

> (**ELISSA** *exits.*)

Clara is a legal resident.

> (**CLARA** *exits.*)

Marisela and Yadira do not have documents.

> (**MARISELA** *and* **YADIRA** *exit.*)

And under current law the two without papers have NO way of becoming citizens. The debate over immigration law is so superficial and so emotional, generally people don't seem to understand the content of the laws they are debating. I want to learn firsthand, what the laws mean and how they affect these young people.

> (**FABIÁN** *and* **JOSEFA** *re-enter the bedroom.*)

FABIÁN. ¡Marisela! Espérenme. No se vayan.

JOSEFA. ¡Diviértanse!

FABIÁN. Yo iba a ir con ella…para protegerla.

YOLANDA. Pues ya se fueron.

JOSEFA. Mi hija.

> (**FABIÁN** *and* **JOSEFA** *look at* **HELEN**.)

FABIÁN. Helen.

HELEN. They grow up so fast. (**HELEN** *makes a sign of growing.*) Muy rápido.

FABIÁN. I want protect her. (**FABIÁN** *exits.*)

HELEN. Don't worry, Josefa. Prom is a rite of passage… It's change.

JOSEFA. Crecer y cambiar es duro. ¡Díle!

YOLANDA. She says change is hard.

JOSEFA. Marisela tenía siete años cuando cruzamos el desierto. Pensé que nos íbamos a morir de calor, de sed, de miedo. ¡Díle!

YOLANDA. When they crossed the desert, Marisela was just seven years old. Josefa thought they were going to die of heat. Thirst. Fear.

HELEN. I have a little son. I can't imagine how scary it would be to walk my little boy across a desert.

JOSEFA. Yo no hablo inglés. No sé leer ni escribir. Y quiero que Marisela nunca trabaje como yo. Quiero que Marisela sea feliz. ¡Díle!

YOLANDA. Josefa can't read or write. She never wants Marisela to do the kind of work she does. She wants Marisela to be happy.

HELEN. I understand… Comprendo.

JOSEFA. Happy. Con permiso. (*Exits.*)

YOLANDA. Do you understand?

HELEN. Yolanda, I am here. I want to understand the world from these girls' perspective.

YOLANDA. So you want to see the world through the eyes of an illegal Latina girl?

HELEN. Yes. I do.

YOLANDA. You're crazy. But good luck with your "reporting," Mrs. John Hickenlooper. (*Exits.*)

HELEN. I prefer Helen Thorpe. *(To the audience.)* I was born in London to Irish parents, who emigrated again, a year later, to the United States. I'm an immigrant. Like the girls, the only country I know is this one. I had to explain words and customs to my parents: like prom and the word sophomore. But I didn't have to translate. I've never had to hide my identity. I've never been considered "illegal". I am drawn to the four girls because we have something in common and we have nothing in common. I wonder if their legal status is beginning to affect how they see one another. More than that, I wonder if their legal status will affect how I see them.

   (A school bell rings.)

And I wonder, is high school for them anything like it was for me?

Scene: High School Classroom

(Projection: Images of a Denver high school: the parking lot, students, front doors. **YADIRA, CLARA,** *and* **ELISSA** *come in in their respective school attire.)*

(Two rows of chairs create the classroom. The **GIRLS** *sit.)*

ANNOUNCER ON THE SPEAKER. Good Morning. Buenos días. Remember class pictures on Friday. Recuerden el viernes se tomarán las fotos de todos los estudiantes.

*(***HELEN*** stumbles in.)*

ELISSA. Helen, sit here.

HELEN. I was just going to hang out and take notes from the back.

CLARA. No, sit next to us.

(The teacher, **MRS. SMITH***, pushes on an overhead projector.)*

MRS. SMITH. QUIET!!! Good morning class. OH! Hello, Ms. Thorpe.

HELEN. Good morning, Mrs. Smith.

MRS. SMITH. Class, we have a very special guest this morning...

HELEN. That's OK, Mrs. Smith; Really, I just want to blend in.

MRS. SMITH. OK!

HELEN. I mean –

---

* A license to produce *Just Like Us* does not include a license to publicly display any third-party or copyrighted images. Licensees must acquire rights for any copyrighted images or create their own.

MRS. SMITH. You don't want to draw attention. I get it. OK. Everyone…Chapter Thirteen, "Convergence and Divergence".

HELEN. *(To* **YADIRA***.)* Where's Marisela?

ELISSA. Marisela won't make it to first period on time today.

CLARA. Her family is moving to another part of town.

HELEN. Why?

ELISSA. Rent's too high at their old place.

MRS. SMITH. Girls please! Quiet down!

CLARA. Mrs. Smith, I was just telling Ms. Thorpe that someone is always moving…to get better rent…better jobs.

MRS. SMITH. Kids change schools all the time, especially at this school.

> *(***MARISELA*** makes a dramatic entrance. And nonchalantly hands in her tardy slip.)*

MARISELA. Not me! I am graduating from this school even if it takes me forty-five minutes to get here.

CLARA. Marisela!

YADIRA. Ya llegó.

ELISSA. Drama Queen!

MARISELA. Oh, Hi Helen.

HELEN. Sit. Sit. I'll stand in the back.

MARISELA. No, Helen… Just scoot over.

> *(***HELEN*** scoots.)*

OK! I'm ready Mrs. Smith.

MRS. SMITH. Marisela, thank you for gracing us with your presence.

MARISELA. I love math, Mrs. Smith.

MR. SMITH. Yes, but apparently you can't tell time.

(Oooh-Ahhhs.)

SMITH. All right, class. Look at the screen:

(Places a transparency on the projector. A complicated calculus problem...we see it appear on the screen behind her.)

Does that converge or diverge?

*(**MARISELA** applies makeup.)*

MARISELA. Diverge.

SMITH. Right. *(Puts up a different equation.)* What about the next one?

MARISELA. Converge.

MRS. SMITH. Correct again. OK, OK, lets see if you can solve this one.

MARISELA. Diverge, again.

(Annoyed? Oohs in the classroom.)

MRS. SMITH. Correct. Again. Marisela, can you please put the makeup away?

MARISELA. Of course, Mrs. Smith.

MRS. SMITH. Gracias, Señorita Benavídez.

MARISELA. ¡De nada!

*(To **HELEN**.)* I really like eyeshadow.

HELEN. *(Smiles.)* I noticed.

MARISELA. Would you like me to do your eyes?

HELEN. Another time.

YADIRA. Careful, she also likes to paint her hair different colors.

MARISELA. What can I say? I'm a colorful woman.

MRS. SMITH. *(Returns to the front of the class.)* Ladies, the test will cover the following: optimization and related rates. And integration.

MARISELA. I love integration.

CLARA. Yo también. Kinda. Sort of.

YADIRA. I think it's hard.

ELISSA. For some people! Ah! *(She high-fives* **MARISELA.***)*

(Bell rings.)

MRS. SMITH. Class dismissed. Remember we have a test on Friday. Friday is the test! Thank you, Ms. Thorpe! It was a pleasure having you in class!

HELEN. Thank you!

Scene: School Hallway/Courtyard

JULIO. *(Young man.)* Hola, Marisela –

MARISELA. Hola, Julio.

JULIO. You did real good in class today.

MARISELA. Ay, gracias, Julio.

JULIO. Your pink? blue? hair...looks nice. OK. Bye.

(Ooohs.)

HELEN. He seems nice.

CLARA. That's the problem. He is! Poor Julio has been in love with Marisela forever.

ELISSA. But she likes older bad boys.

MARISELA. I'm a very mature woman.

ELISSA. Ha!

CLARA. Yadira, on the other hand, has been with her boyfriend for three years. It's like they're already married.

YADIRA. I'm never getting married.

HELEN. Why not?

YADIRA. You know what they call husband and wife in Spanish? Esposo/esposa. Which is the word for handcuff. Ugh.

CLARA. Not all men are like your dad. Or your stepfather.

ELISSA. Clara, what do you know about men?

HELEN. Do you have a boyfriend, Clara?

CLARA. *(Giggles flustered.)* Me? ¡Ay, no!

ELISSA. She's too shy. And I'm too picky. I don't have time for a real boyfriend.

(**ANA** *walks on.*)

ANA. Hi! Marisela!

MARISELA. Hola, Ana.

ANA. Did you hear the great news? I gots me some free money for college!!!

MARISELA. That's great.

ANA. Seven thousand dollars from the Daniels Fund to go to the University of Colorado. What about you, Marisela?

MARISELA. I haven't checked the mail yet.

ANA. Who's the Lady? Are you in trouble?

MARISELA. Oh! Ana, I'd like you to meet my mother... Elena.

ANA. What? No way. She can't be your mother!

HELEN. Why not?

ANA. Ah, cause you are so...so...

HELEN. Short? *(Whatever adjective fits the actor.)*

ANA. Yeah, and Marisela is so CHEDDAR!

(**ANA** *dashes off.* **MARISELA** *gets mad!)*

MARISELA. Cheddar! ¡Que qué! Did you hear what she called me?

ELISSA. You were gonna make poor Helen your Mom!

HELEN. I'd be honored.

MARISELA. Nah, you wouldn't. But seriously –

YADIRA. Seriously! Did you hear? Ana got seven thousand dollars? She's always asking me for the answers!

HELEN. I take it Ana is not a friend.

MARISELA. Not to me; Ana is (Friends with the) Chicana(s). She assumes I also applied to the Daniels Fund.

ELISSA. You can't anymore! You have to have a social security card now!

HELEN. Wait! Slow down. When you say Chicana...what does that mean for you?

YADIRA. For me, Chicana is someone who was born here.

CLARA. She probably doesn't even speak Spanish.

ELISSA. And the Chicanas usually don't like los Mexicanos.

CLARA. Except Julio. He's Chicano and he loves you!

MARISELA. Yeah, but some of the other Chicanos, they call us names.

HELEN. Names? Like what?

ELISSA. Like ched or cheddar...

HELEN. Like cheddar cheese?

*(The **GIRLS** laugh.)*

ELISSA. No. Like from Ranchera as in Ranchera music.

CLARA. The country music lots of Mexicans like.

MARISELA. Especially Northern Mexicans. Like me.

(The girls sing a song in the style of "El Rey" by José Alfredo Jiménez.)*

MARISELA. Oh, that is a great old song. It goes "With money or without money, I still do what I want."

---

* A license to produce *Just Like Us* does not include a performance license for "El Rey" by José Alfredo Jiménez. The publisher and author suggest that the licensee contact ASCAP or BMI to ascertain the music publisher and contact such music publisher to license or acquire permission for performance of the song. If a license or permission is unattainable for "El Rey" the licensee may not use the song in *Just Like Us* but should create an original composition in a similar style or use a similar song in the public domain. For further information, please see the Music and Third-Party Materials Use Note on page iii.

YADIRA. If Ana heard from the Daniels Fund, you guys must have heard too!

MARISELA. So did you?

ELISSA. Yes. *(Beat.)* I got a full ride to Regis University!

>   *(Glee. They hug her.)*

MARISELA. ¿Y tú, Clara?

CLARA. *(Pulls out an envelope.)* I'm too scared to open it.

YADIRA. You should open it, Clara.

MARISELA. Yes, you should.

>   *(The **GIRLS** chant "Open it! Open it" or "Ábrelo, ábrelo." **CLARA** opens it.)*

CLARA. It says that at the University of Denver tuition is forty thousand dollars.

YADIRA. ¡Válgame! ¿Tanto así?

ELISSA. How much is the Daniels Fund giving you?

CLARA. Ay! I got the whole thing!

>   *(Glee.)*

YADIRA.	ELISSA.
Wow, Clara!	¡Qué padre!

HELEN. That is great news, Clara. Congratulations Elissa!

ELISSA. We are going to college, Clara!

>   *(The **TWO GIRLS** hug. **YADIRA** and **MARISELA** look at each other.)*

CLARA. I'm sorry girls. I can't help but be happy.

YADIRA. You both worked so hard.

ELISSA. Thank you.

CLARA. But so do you.

YADIRA. Girls, this is great news.

MARISELA. We are happy for you. Congratulations!

MRS. SMITH. Girls, what's all the noise about?

MARISELA. Clara and Elissa got full rides to college!

MRS. SMITH. *(High fives.)* All right, I see you! Hey, all that extra work was worth it!

> *(The bell rings. The* **GIRLS** *take their books and book bags and close their lockers.)*

Scene: The Courtyard

(They all cross to a bench.)

HELEN. Why do you think you got this money?

CLARA. I'm a good student.

ELISSA. I do a lot of extracurriculars.

CLARA. I wrote a good essay.

CLARA & ELISSA. I'm Latina. Jinx!

YADIRA. Latinas, and you have papers.

HELEN. Who is the best student out of the four of you?

ALL. Marisela.

MARISELA. But it doesn't matter.

CLARA. Funny thing, we grew up believing we were equals.

ELISSA. *(Correcting* **CLARA.***)* We are equals. I mean I know I'm a citizen, but I'm just as American and just as Mexican as Yadira and Marisela.

CLARA. And each of us has a parent who entered the country illegally.

ELISSA. And none of our parents can help us pay for college.

MARISELA. Except I wanted to get a driver's license and I couldn't. So I started driving with a fake Mexican license. And that's when I realized I was going to grow up doing every thing the wrong way.

CLARA. Without a license you can't open a checking account, get a credit card, or even rent a movie!

YADIRA. We couldn't go on the National Honors Society trip to DC.

MARISELA. No. We don't have IDs to get on the plane.

ELISSA. We've all gone to the same school! We get good grades.

YADIRA. But we don't have the same chances.

MARISELA. Do you think I'll get to go to college, Helen?

HELEN. I certainly hope so.

MARISELA. Do you think anyone out there will care if I don't go?

HELEN. I don't know. But you will.

Scene: The Recruiter

(*A* **RECRUITER** *walks in.*)

RECRUITER. Excuse me, I'm looking for Yadira Vargas.

ELISSA. This is Yadira Vargas.

MARISELA. OH-oh.

YADIRA. Elissa!

RECRUITER. May I speak with you?

YADIRA. Helen, come with me. Please.

HELEN. Why? What can I...?

MARISELA. You're white. He's white. (*Or.*) You're Gringa...
He's Gringo.

ELISSA. Help her.

CLARA. Protect her.

MARISELA. He might be Immigration. Go!

HELEN. Hello. I'm Helen Thorpe, a friend of Yadira's.

RECRUITER. You look very familiar, Helen.

(**HELEN** *goes over and shakes the* **RECRUITER***'s
hand.* **YADIRA** *follows.*)

MARISELA. Elissa, what were you thinking pointing Yadira
out like that?

CLARA. He looks awfully official.

ELISSA. I'm sorry. I just didn't think...

MARISELA. You have your papers, you don't think like
we do!

RECRUITER. Nice to meet you both. Yadira, my name is
Tom Johnson.

HELEN. Is there a problem?

RECRUITER. No! Not at all! I am with the University of Colorado. It's come to my attention that you, Yadira, have an impressive ACT score.

YADIRA. Oh. Oh! Thank you.

HELEN. That's good news.

RECRUITER. What classes are you taking this semester?

YADIRA. AP Chemistry, AP Calculus, AP English and Spanish. My GPA is 4.0.

RECRUITER. Excellent! Here's my card. We would really like for you to consider applying to University of Colorado.

YADIRA. Really? Do you have scholarships?

RECRUITER. For a girl with your grades we certainly do. Have you filled in your Federal Student Aid Forms yet?

YADIRA. No. *(Beat.)* I can't. I got a problem. A really big problem. *(Beat.)* I don't have papers.

RECRUITER. Oh. Well, now I have a problem. University of Colorado is a public university...I can't "knowingly" recruit an undocumented student.

YADIRA. Oh God. Please don't turn me into Immigration. I don't know anyone in Mexico.

RECRUITER. Yadira, I would never consider it part of my job to report you. We have a "Don't ask, don't tell," kind of policy.

YADIRA. All my life, I've worked so I could go to college. I would make you proud.

RECRUITER. You could apply as an "international student from Mexico". But we can't waive your application fee... and unfortunately we can't guarantee any scholarships or get you financial aid, or federal Pell grants.

YADIRA. My stepfather is a full-time janitor. My mother sorts clothes for Goodwill. Together they make seventeen thousand dollars a year. That's why I need help. I don't want to end up in jobs like theirs.

RECRUITER. Yadira, I'm very sorry. *(Shakes **YADIRA**'s hand and **HELEN**'s hand.)* Good luck.

> *(**RECRUITER** exits.)*

MARISELA. Who was that?

HELEN. It was a recruiter.

CLARA. Yadira, that's great!

YADIRA. Not if you're me. I'm poor. I'm illegal.

ELISSA. Don't call yourself that.

YADIRA. The teachers say Live the American Dream! Study! Everybody who studies hard can go to college. But that's not true. I can't raise my hand and say, I don't have my papers. It's not clear who you can trust. I'm less than all of you. And you know it! A part of me is saying you have to go to class. And another is saying "Screw it – I give up!"

ELISSA. C'mon Yadira. You can't give up. Not now.

> *(**ELISSA** and **CLARA** follow **YADIRA** out.)*

MARISELA. Helen, write this down. We started working at King Soopers when we were thirteen. We go to school eight a.m. to three p.m. We work from four to eleven for minimum wage – Yadira and I pay taxes on that money that we can never claim. We do our homework after that. We are at the top of our classes. But we still can't pay for college.

HELEN. So, let me play Devil's Advocate. You aren't even supposed to be in the U.S. You've already received a free education through high school. Maybe striving for more is...too much to hope for. What good does it do our nation to invest in someone who doesn't have the right to be here?

MARISELA. What good does it do ANY nation for me to be poor, desperate and uneducated? I'm here. College is my American Dream. I could really contribute. Be a doctor. A good doctor.

HELEN. You would make a good lawyer.

MARISELA. I do like to argue.

HELEN. So go to community college!

MARISELA. Get this. Community college costs three times more for kids like us. Plus we can't get Pell grants or loans. It's crazy the only hope for Yadira and me is a private scholarship for a private college.

HELEN. How does that make you feel?

MARISELA. It's like Yadira and I were branded with a big red letter "I" for ILLEGAL when we were little kids. And we try to hide it, but it's always there. Nothing good we do will ever make it go away.

    (MARISELA *exits.)*

HELEN. And suddenly I am staring to feel that this story might need to be a bit longer than two columns in a magazine.

Scene: The Tattered Cover Bookstore

*(A small crowd has gathered. **TOM TANCREDO** takes the podium. He is grounded and affable. Very folksy.)*

TANCREDO. My name is Tom Tancredo, Congressman from Littleton, Colorado. I understand why people want to come here. I do. I am a grandchild of immigrants! My grandfather came here from Italy as a poor orphan. And it was not easy. But he never flew an Italian flag, only an American one, and he constantly talked about the importance of becoming Americanized. You know, I taught in the school district for years...and they started insisting that we start teaching in Spanish. You know what my Italian grandfather would say to that? "Speak American damn it!"

(Clapping.)

HELEN. Tom Tancredo, affable, smart, folksy and one of the nation's most vehement Representatives against illegal immigration.

TOM. Listen, this is not a message of exclusion: it's a message of inclusion. Nobody is excluded in the U.S. because of their race, color or creed. All we ask is that you actually in your heart become an American. Cut all ties with the old. Connect with America! And if you have a language other than English, then it's got to go. The U.S. is a nation of immigrants, but they must be immigrants who honor and uphold our laws. Who act and speak like real Americans. God bless! Thank you!

(Clapping.)

HELEN. As I listen to him speak, I wonder: How did a minor Representative from a minor district in Colorado become a major spokesman on immigration?

And when did immigration move from being a regional concern to becoming such a hot-topic issue in national politics?

The last big national discussion happened in the mid-eighties, when President Ronald Regan, issued pardons through a lottery for immigrants without documentation.

So what suddenly catapulted the issue to the national consciousness?

(Projected pictures of the 9/11 hijackers appear on the screens.)*

The girls were high school sophomores when nineteen men – all of whom had entered the United States *legally* using nonimmigrant travel visas – hijacked four jetliners and flew them at various targets including the World Trade Center.

This unprecedented attack on U.S. soil, prompted a slew of legislation to increase security, tighten our borders, and make the American people feel safer from foreign influences. The INS became a part of Homeland Security. Suddenly, any immigrant was a potential type of terrorist, and although we knew most weren't violent, the fear of them undermining our language and American way of life became a palpable fear on the political stage.

---

* A license to produce *Just Like Us* does not include a license to publicly display any third-party or copyrighted images. Licensees must acquire rights for any copyrighted images or create their own.

Scene: Back at School

(The **GIRLS** *enter.* **CLARA** *is holding a newspaper.)*

CLARA. Girls, look! *The Denver Post* just did a story about a star student in high school: He doesn't have papers and is struggling to go to college and a donor decided to pay his tuition.

ELISSA. Jesús Apodaca.

CLARA. He's so cute!

ELISSA. He looks smart.

YADIRA. He can't be that smart. He let the *Post* take his picture and use his real name.

MARISELA. I bet Tom Tancredo and his Republican friends go after Jesús.

(Light on **TOM TANCREDO**.*)*

TOM TANCREDO. – *The Denver Post* brazenly publicizes an illegal student on the front page and nobody reports him for deportation? Now, I'm sure Jesús Apodaca is a nice kid. It's great he's hard working and smart. But he should use his smarts to improve things in Mexico where he legally belongs. I am calling the Department of Homeland Security tonight to report Jesús and his family for deportation.

*(*TANCREDO *exits.)*

HELEN. You know, Immigration is so complicated; you can't assume it's simply a partisan issue. Did you notice who funded Jesus Apodaca's scholarship?

YADIRA. *(Reads the article.)* The donor is a Republican "who admires Apodaca's entrepreneurship and can-do spirit."

HELEN. Yes. And a Republican co-sponsored the DREAM Act, which would give undocumented students who graduate high school the chance to go to college and start a pathway to citizenship.

MARISELA. Órale!

CLARA. There's hope, girls.

ELISSA. Real hope.

MARISELA. Damn, when's the last time the newspaper had good news?

CLARA. Maybe we should read *The Denver Post* more often.

(The **GIRLS** *exit…* **YADIRA** *lags.)*

Scene: Yadira's Story

HELEN. Yadira...are you OK?

> (**YADIRA** *pulls out her dance clothes and starts to change.*)

YADIRA. I just don't get so hopeful like the rest of them.

HELEN. You know, if the DREAM Act passes, you could call that recruiter. You could get a scholarship to a public University. You would be on the road to becoming a bonafide American.

YADIRA. But, Helen, in so many ways I'm already an American. I don't have one single memory of Mexico. My whole life has happened in the States.

When I was little, my mom, submitted an application for citizenship through my dad, but when he left us... it became void. My mom was alone, with no English, raising me and my little sister Zulema. I went to five different elementary schools.

HELEN. Was your sister born here?

YADIRA. Yes. Zulema coughs, and she's off to the doctor because she has Medicaid. But I'm having the flu, and we don't go. But I go to school. I get good grades. But my options are running out.

HELEN. What if someone from *The Denver Post* wrote about you?

YADIRA. No. No way. I don't want a gang of politicians outside my door trying to deport me.

HELEN. Listen Yadira...if you want things to change, the debate has to deepen and people need to understand the whole situation. I know some writers at *The Denver Post* that would agree not to use your name or take your picture.

YADIRA. OK. If you think it might help other kids like me. I'll do it.

> (**YADIRA** *exits. We see* The Post *article on the screens.**)

HELEN. *(To the audience.)* An enraged Tom Tancredo and his people, who hounded Jesús Apodaca's family until they moved in the middle of the night, are not able to uncover Yadira's identity. The article is opening doors for Yadira.

---

* A license to produce *Just Like Us* does not include a license to publicly display any third-party or copyrighted images. Licensees must acquire rights for any copyrighted images or create their own.

Scene: Cynthia Poundstone

(CYNTHIA POUNDSTONE *enters.)*

HELEN. Yadira, this is Cynthia Poundstone. She's a local fundraiser who read the article and wants to meet you.

YADIRA. *(Poised.)* Hello Ms. Poundstone, nice to meet you.

POUNDSTONE. Yadira. I am an alumna of Whittier College and we can use a bright girl like you. I have talked to the director of admissions and based on your grades and accomplishments they would like to offer you admission and a partial scholarship. If you accept, I will galvanize a group of people to raise the rest.

YADIRA. Thank you... Where's Whittier College?

POUNDSTONE. In California.

YADIRA. Wow. That's so far away.

POUNDSTONE. Let's fly you there. Show you around.

HELEN. Cynthia... Yadira, doesn't have an ID. She can't fly.

POUNDSTONE. No matter, you'll take the bus.

HELEN. There are now federal searches on buses too. *(Beat.)* It's just too risky.

POUNDSTONE. *(Handing* **YADIRA** *an impressive folder from Whittier College.)* I hope you will take a leap of faith and just accept.

YADIRA. Thank you very much.

(POUNDSTONE *exits.* **MARISELA** *enters.)*

MARISELA. Yadira, the talent show is about to start. And... wait what's that?

YADIRA. An envelope

MARISELA. With your name?

YADIRA. Whittier accepted me…and gave me a partial scholarship. And Ms. Poundstone is raising the rest. *(Happiness.)*

MARISELA. Are you taking it?

YADIRA. I should. But leave my Mom? My sister? You? I'm still hoping on Mr. Mesquita at the University of Denver. He's says our applications look very good. My dream is you and I both get in, get the money…and we go to college…together…here!!!

MARISELA. That's not going to happen for me.

YADIRA. Why not? You get better grades than I do; you are at the top of our class

MARISELA. It doesn't matter. I'm too "colorful".

YADIRA. I don't have pink hair if that's what you mean.

MARISELA. Your accent is less strong. You seem less foreign. I am more loud and scarier. I seem more Mexican.

YADIRA. I don't even know what that means anymore. Marisela – this isn't about the way you look.

MARISELA. We were in this together. We were the unequals. The illegals. But now, you get in *The Denver Post*. You are going to school. You are getting a scholarship

YADIRA. It's just luck, Marisela.

HELEN. I'm sorry, I didn't mean for this to be a problem.

MARISELA. I'm sorry, Helen. I'm happy for you, Yadira. I really am. It's just… It's just…

*(**CLARA** and **ELISSA** enter.)*

ELISSA. Girls – the talent show! The talent show! Ya mero nos toca. We gotta get backstage!

CLARA. Your mother is here.

MARISELA. She is? I thought she had to work.

ELISSA. And that recruiter from DU just walked in too.

YADIRA & MARISELA. CÉZAR MESQUITA??

MARISELA. Why didn't you say that!

ELISSA. I just did.

CLARA. I bet he has good news for both of you!

MARISELA. This is it! *(She hugs* **YADIRA.***)* Cézar Mesquita is here.

YADIRA. Fingers crossed, amiga.

MARISELA. Girls, let's go.

Scene: The Talent Show

(A crowd including **CÉZAR MESQUITA** *and* **JOSEFA** *is gathered to watch the Senior Talent Show.)*

PRINCIPAL. *(Voice-over.)* Thank you! Let's hear it for the dynamic duo Sonny and Charro! Now for the last number of Roosevelt High's Senior Talent Show, Las Adelitas de Denver.

ALL. Five, six, seven, eight!

(The first beats of a song like Lenny Kravitz's "American Woman"...the girls dance. Then *the dance moves change from rock, hip-hop, to Latino Cumbia...the crowd goes wild.)*

PRINCIPAL. *(Voice-over.)* Thank you for coming, ¡Muchas gracias!

(In the background, **CÉZAR MESQUITA** *finds* **YADIRA** *and talks to her. It is good news.)*

MARISELA. Mami, ¿Se acuerda de Helen?

JOSEFA. Si. ¿Como estás Helen?

HELEN. Muchos saludos, Josefa.

JOSEFA. Dale con el español, Helen!

*(***JULIO*** approaches.)*

---

* A license to produce *Just Like Us* does not include a performance license for "American Woman" by Lenny Kravitz. The publisher and author suggest that the licensee contact ASCAP or BMI to ascertain the music publisher and contact such music publisher to license or acquire permission for performance of the song. If a license or permission is unattainable for "American Woman", the licensee may not use the song in *Just Like Us* but should create an original composition in a similar style or use a similar song in the public domain. For further information, please see the Music and Third-Party Materials Use Note on page iii.

JULIO. Hola, Señora, Ms. Thorpe.

ALL. Hola, Julio.

JULIO. You dance real good, Marisela.

MARISELA. Ay. Gracias, Julio.

JULIO. OK. Bye. *(Exits.)*

JOSEFA. That Julio – good boy.

MARISELA. Ay, Mami. Did you like the dance?

JOSEFA. Siento que fue un poco movido.

MARISELA. Ay, mamá.

Mr. Mesquita! I saw you! I was hoping you would come talk to me.

CÉZAR. You were great in the dance. Congratulations.

MARISELA. Thank you. Mi Mami, Helen: this is Cézar Mesquita, director of diversity enrollment for DU: The University of Denver. It's a private school.

HELEN. Nice to meet you.

CÉZAR. Mucho gusto, Helen, Señora Benavidez.

MARISELA. Mr. Mesquita, are you going to be able to help me go to college?

CÉZAR. Marisela...you are accepted to DU.

MARISELA. I am!? That's wonderful! With a scholarship?

CÉZAR. It is very competitive, and I'm afraid the private donor has not elected to sponsor you.

MARISELA. What? Why?

CÉZAR. You are an exceptional candidate but a private scholarship is at the discretion of the person who funds it.

MARISELA. This is it. My last chance. My life without a college degree?!! It looks bad: working at King Soopers forever, or marrying young, just to get out of the house. My dad – he cleans stores alone at night. My mother cleans houses. It's not what they want for me.

CÉZAR. I'm sorry. I wish it were different.

(**CÉZAR** *exits.* **YADIRA** *and* **GIRLS** *approach.*)

MARISELA. Mami! Mami!

(**JOSEFA** *hugs her.*)

JOSEFA. ¿Qué pasó? ¿Qué pasó? ¿Por qué lloras, mi hija?

MARISELA. Me aceptaron en la universidad, pero no gané la beca.

JOSEFA. Voy a guardar dinero suficiente para la escuela de belleza.

MARISELA. ¡Mami! I don't want to go to Beauty School. I want to do something with my head, not other people's hair.

JOSEFA. Es tarde. Tengo que ir a trabajar.

MARISELA. You have to go work. Thanks for coming.

JOSEFA. Nos vemos en la casa. Ten ánimo.

(**JOSEFA** *exits.* **YADIRA** *approaches.*)

MARISELA. You got it, huh?

YADIRA. Yes.

MARISELA. *(Shakes her head.)* So now you can go to DU.

YADIRA. *(Very sad.)* I guess so.

MARISELA. Or Whittier!

YADIRA. Marisela, please stop.

HELEN. Marisela, I'm so sorry.

MARISELA. I've worked so hard. What's wrong with me?

(She exits, the **GIRLS** *follow.)*

HELEN. *(To the audience.)* This Spring, thousands of young promising students – like Marisela – find their chances of going to college or the army getting dimmer and dimmer as the Senate debates, argues, fights and stalls the DREAM Act. And I'm suddenly left wondering, is there something wrong with us?

Scene: High School Graduation

(Projection: Images of a high school graduation. "Pomp and Circumstance" plays.)*

(The **GIRLS** *enter in their caps and gowns.)*

MARISELA. Please be seated. My name is Marisela Benavidez and I am proud to be this year's Valedictorian. There were more than six hundred students in my freshman class; now only two hundred thirty-five seniors are preparing to graduate. Nobody at Roosevelt High can say exactly what happened to the other four hundred students who were once here. They moved away, dropped out, fell through the cracks. We are the survivors. We are here. We are graduating.

(Applause.)

Those of you going to college...I want you to realize how special you are. How talented you are. And how proud we are of you. You are "nuestra esperanza" – our hope for the future.

ELISSA. Stop! This is not right.

(Big light shift.)

CLARA. We have to help Marisela.

YADIRA. There has to be a way.

POUNDSTONE. How can I help?

GIRLS. Ms. Poundstone!

---

* A license to produce *Just Like Us* does not include a performance license for any third-party or copyrighted recordings, or a license to publicly display any third-party or copyrighted images. Licensees must also acquire rights for any copyrighted images or create their own. For further information, please see the Music and Third-Party Materials Use Note on page iii.

YADIRA. I can't believe I am saying this...but – could the money you raised for me for Whittier...maybe go to Marisela so she can go to DU too?

MARISELA. What?

POUNDSTONE. I would have to convince the donors, but they're gonna love Marisela!

HELEN. Marisela, you're halfway there!

ELISSA. We need to find another twenty thousand dollars for DU.

MARISELA. That's a lot of money. How are we going to raise that?

CÉZAR. I'll help you.

GIRLS. Mr. Mesquita!

CÉZAR. – I'm going to get you a ten thousand dollar scholarship.

MRS. SMITH. I'll help you, too Marisela.

GIRLS. Mrs. Smith!

MRS. SMITH. I will talk to every business owner in the community and we'll raise the money you need for college.

MARISELA. ¡Gracias! Thank you! I'm going to college. I'm going to college!

PRINCIPAL. *(Voice-over.)* Graduates, congratulations!

(Glee and hugs. Now the hats go up in the air.)

Scene: Mexico Alive in the US

(Ranchera music and a party. The* **GIRLS** *take off their gowns, hand them to* **JOSEFA** *and are at the party. Mexico comes alive in the Benavídez's small backyard. Card tables with tamales and barbacoa. There is a piñata. The* **GIRLS** *sing the "Dale, Dale" song and blindfold each other as they take swings.)*

POUNDSTONE. Get a picture, Helen!

(The **GIRLS** *get their party to pose with them.)*

HELEN. Say Cheese!

GIRLS. Cheddar!

(A flash.)

HELEN. *(To* **CYNTHIA.***)* What do you think? Should Marisela and Yadira live together next year?

MARISELA & YADIRA. Together. Together!

HELEN. Or should they branch out and live with other people?

MARISELA & YADIRA. No! No!

CYNTHIA. I think the support they can give each other is going to be important.

MARISELA. Hear, that Yadira. You gotta support me. ¡Aunque no me aguantes!

---

* A license to produce *Just Like Us* does not include a performance license for any third-party or copyrighted music. Licensees should create an original composition or use music in the public domain. For further information, please see the Music and Third-Party Materials Use Note on page iii.

POUNDSTONE. College is not an easy place. Only one in ten Latina girls finishes a four year degree. It's easy to get overwhelmed and drop out.

YADIRA. Not us! No matter how hard it is, we'll never drop out.

CLARA. I'm so excited.

ELISSA. Me too. We did it, girls!

MARISELA. We did it! Together!

(*The* **GIRLS** *hug, then start dancing.*)

POUNDSTONE. Oh, Helen. Put down your notebook. You need a drink. (*Hands her a little tequila.*)

HELEN. They have been friends for a long time. I hope that continues.

POUNDSTONE. Me too ¡Salud!

HELEN. ¡Salud!

Scene: Getting Ready For College

(The **GIRLS** *pull out suitcases, open them, pull out jeans, put them on, pull off their dresses, put on college sweatshirts. Music... The* **GIRLS** *hug.* **ELISSA** *waves and exits for college.)*

HELEN. *(To the audience.)* Elissa, our American citizen, is the first one to leave as she embarks for Regis University. Once at school, she drifts apart from the other girls...and their friendship ends.

(The **OTHER GIRLS** *continue to pack.)*

Clara, Yadira, and Marisela get ready to leave for DU.

*(***CLARA** *and* **YADIRA** *exit.* **JOSEFA** *and* **FABIÁN** *come in.)*

JOSEFA & FABIÁN. ¡Marisela, no te vas a ir!

MARISELA. What do you mean I can't go?

FABIÁN. ¡No puedes vivir en la Universidad!

MARISELA. Papi! Mami! I have to live in the dorms!

JOSEFA. ¿Qué con los muchachos?...No.

MARISELA. Boys won't be a problem!

FABIÁN. No quiero que se te olvide quién eres, de dónde vienes...y lo que es verdaderamente importante, la familia.

MARISELA. Papi – I know family is the most important thing.

FABIÁN. Entonces, hija, quédate aquí, viviendo con nosotros. *(He grabs her bag.)*

MARISELA. No Papi. I can't stay at home... I'm going to DU. I'm living in the dorms, just like everyone else!

FABIÁN. Estoy harto de esta escuincla americana! Y también de esa pinche gringa!

> *(Frustrated,* **FABIÁN** *exits.* **MARISELA** *and* **HELEN** *and* **JOSEFA** *are alone on stage.)*

HELEN. Why are they upset, Marisela?

MARISELA. *(To* **HELEN**.*)* They envision me out on the street, living out of control with boys and I don't know what! I've been getting more independent and they don't like it.

JOSEFA. Helen, en mi pueblo, las muchachas se quedan en casa hasta que encuentran marido. Home. Díle!

MARISELA. In her hometown, girls live with their parents until they find a man. What she doesn't say, is she got married at sixteen. I know this is what they want for me. But college is so foreign to them.

HELEN. Josefa, I understand, when I went to college my mom cried every day for a month.

> *(***JOSEFA** *hugs* **MARISELA**.*)*

JOSEFA. No te quiero perder.

MARISELA. *(Beat.)* Ah, Mami, You're not losing me. No te apures. I'll be careful. I want to be somebody.

> *(***MARISELA** *kneels.)*

Dame la bendición, Amá.

JOSEFA. *(Broken-hearted.)* Que Dios te bendiga, hija.

> *(***JOSEFA** *makes the sign of the cross on her daughter.)*

Helen – por favor, protect her.

> *(***JOSEFA** *exits, crying.)*

HELEN. *(To the audience.)* And so Marisela, the first of her family to ever go beyond the sixth grade, moves out of her house, away from her Latino neighborhood, from the panaderías, and taco stands, hair salons, and travels ten miles south to the other side of the world, to the more affluent whiter neighborhood that will become her new home: the University of Denver.

And I wonder if any of us are prepared for what lies ahead.

ACT TWO

Scene: University of Denver Dorm Room

*(Latino music. Projection: Images of campus.**
We see the **GIRLS** *studying in their room.*
HELEN *is there.)*

HELEN. It's October. The girls are adjusting to college, and I am adjusting to "hanging out" in a corner of their dorm.

*(***HELEN*** *sits on a bean bag or chair.* **MARISELA** *enters in a bathrobe.)*

MARISELA. Hey, Brownies! Be Brownies!

YADIRA & CLARA. Go, Brownies!

HELEN. Brownies?

*(***GIRLS*** *touch their skin.)*

GIRLS. Brownies!!!

MARISELA. Clara, have you already finished the Social Equity homework?

CLARA. I don't want to get behind!

YADIRA. Social Equity! Yeah, right.

MARISELA. Yadira, are you OK?

YADIRA. A student in the cafeteria handed me her dirty tray...and thanked me for making her food.

MARISELA. No way!

CLARA. She was very sweet about it.

MARISELA. What did you say?

YADIRA. I didn't know what to say. So I smiled and took the tray to the kitchen.

CLARA. Did you know that Julio's uncle works back there? He says Julio sends his love.

MARISELA. Ay! Poor Julio.

YADIRA. The only people that look like us here are the cafeteria workers, the cleaning staff, and the security guards.

CLARA. More Brownies!

MARISELA. Oh, there's someone else, Ladies! And he's moving in with us. Manuel Landeta!

HELEN. Manuel Landeta?

MARISELA. Mexico's hottest telenovela star!

CLARA. Hot? He's like forty years old!

MARISELA. I think we should celebrate our heritage and hang up his poster right by our Mexican flag!

> *(She unrolls a poster. Perhaps it's projected on screen.)*

YADIRA. ¡Ay no! That's simply unacceptable.

CLARA. ¡Ay no! That's much too much!

YADIRA. He's wearing much too little.

MARISELA. I like him. Don't you, Helen? He's a gentleman. (*Shows her the poster.*)

HELEN. I don't know any gentlemen who oil their bodies.

YADIRA. Marisela, No!

(**LUCY** *knocks on the door.*)

LUCY. Hey, girls! It's me.

CLARA. Dios mio! Put that poster away. It's Lucy! From my Bible study.

MARISELA. She will love it!

CLARA. (*Opens door.*) Hi, Lucy.

LUCY. Hey, Clara, your roommate told me you were hanging with your "homies".

MARISELA. I guess that's us.

YADIRA. Hey, Lucy!

LUCY. Hi! Oh, excuse me, Ma'am. I don't think we've met (*Shakes her hand.*) Are you with the Resident Life?

HELEN. Me? Oh no. I'm Helen...

CLARA. She's a...

MARISELA.	**YADIRA**.
Reporter	Kind of sort of...friend of ours.

LUCY. Friend? Reporting on what? Ma'am?

HELEN. Well –

MARISELA. Just on how cool girls like us...enjoy college.

HELEN. Something like that. Nice to meet you, Lucy.

LUCY. Likewise, Ma'am.

*(**LUCY** spots a picture on the desk.)*

LUCY. Hey this is a picture of you girls! You look so pretty, Clarita!

CLARA. Thanks... It's our graduation party. At Marisela's house.

LUCY. Really? Is that your house?

MARISELA. Yeah. Is something wrong with it?

LUCY. Why do you have bars on your windows?

CLARA. All the houses on Umatilla Street do.

*(The **GIRLS** look at each other.)*

LUCY. I don't get it. Why would you live in a place like that?

MARISELA. *(Beat.)* Lucy... I have a secret to tell you.

YADIRA. Marisela, no –

MARISELA. We all live in places like that because...we are poor.

CLARA & YADIRA. Marisela!

LUCY. What do you mean, poor?

MARISELA. Poor: it means our parents don't make a lot of money.

YADIRA. Enough! Marisela, don't be mean.

MARISELA. It's true. I don't know why we act so ashamed of it all the time. The biggest class in America is working class.

LUCY. Where did you hear that?

MARISELA. Today. In college.

LUCY. You know. My great grandfather was a plumber. From Germany. And we all know Jesus was a carpenter.

MARISELA. Lucy, *we* are *below* working class: We are the working poor.

CLARA. Marisela!

YADIRA. You don't need to air all our laundry.

HELEN. Why is talking about income so hard to do?

LUCY. It's considered rude.

HELEN. But it's, more than that. What is it?

YADIRA. Because it's like saying, I'm worth this much.

MARISELA. Everybody wants to have some class.

LUCY. Yeah, I'd love to be fancy. We are totally middle class.

YADIRA. How do you know?

LUCY. Because like we go skiing but my dad still complains and says its costs an arm and a leg. So we do nice things, but we still have to budget.

HELEN. If you don't mind me asking, how much do your parents make?

LUCY. Around three hundred thousand dollars a year.

MARISELA. Lucy, that's not middle class.

LUCY. It's not? But I feel so average.

MARISELA. You know this course we are all taking has really opened my eyes.

CLARA. It's embarrassing.

MARISELA. It's not embarrassing. It's wrong. My family earns twenty thousand dollars a year. And my family has six people.

LUCY. How is that possible?

MARISELA. Easy. All you do is: multiply hours worked times the minimum wage. And then subtract taxes.

LUCY. What is the minimum wage right now?

MARISELA, CLARA & YADIRA. Five-fifteen an hour.

LUCY. But you can barely get a cup of coffee with that.

YADIRA. Have you ever had a job, Lucy?

LUCY. No. I'm sorry. I go to school, that's my job. I was a counselor at Bible camp. I didn't get paid...but that was a lot of work.

CLARA. Lucy, you don't have to defend yourself. Maybe we should stop this.

LUCY. No, this is OK. I mean this is why I came to college. Right? To learn.

YADIRA. Yes, us too.

HELEN. Girls, what's prompting all of this?

YADIRA. We are taking a social equity class with Professor Martínez.

MARISELA. It's awesome.

LUCY. That's funny. Social equity is not a requirement for business majors.

YADIRA. Well, maybe it should be.

LUCY. So you are poor?

MARISELA. Income wise, yes.

LUCY. My father always said that people are poor because they just don't work hard enough.

MARISELA. Really? You think my dad scrubbing floors all night isn't hard work?

LUCY. Your dad scrubs floors for a living?

MARISELA. Yes.

HELEN. So your dad says one thing. What do you think, Lucy?

LUCY. I don't know. That maybe hard-working people shouldn't be poor.

MARISELA. Lucy, I totally agree.

LUCY. You know what my father says the main problem is?

MARISELA. Lack of education?

LUCY. No. Illegal immigration.

MARISELA. *(Beat.)* Illegal immigration?

LUCY. Right! My father says illegal immigrants are killing this nation. That's why so many people are poor! Because illegal immigrant stole jobs, now your poor dad is forced to clean floors at night.

MARISELA. Oh.

LUCY. You're nice. You work hard. I don't want you to be poor. Aren't you tired of people assuming you are an illegal alien simply because you are of Mexican descent? That must be an awful feeling.

MARISELA. It is.

LUCY. Don't you think we should stop the aliens?

MARISELA. Aliens?

LUCY. From breaking the law? And hurting you? The government should secure the borders so we can all have better jobs. And illegals should apply to be American citizens like they ought to.

(*Silence.*)

HELEN. Lucy, if you came here illegally, there's no way of staying and becoming legal...there's no way to become a citizen.

LUCY. Aren't there applications? I saw that movie *Green Card*. You can also marry a citizen and become a citizen.

HELEN. Not anymore, Lucy. The law changed.

YADIRA. The system is broken.

CLARA. What if I had come over here illegally?

LUCY. Clara. You are such a good girl. You wouldn't break the law.

MARISELA. Ay Dios mio.

CLARA. Even so...but what if I had come over illegally?

LUCY. I would be scared to be your friend.

CLARA. *(Hurt.)* Scared?

LUCY. You would be breaking the law. There might be people coming after you. Worse, you would have lied to me. I couldn't trust you.

CLARA. What if my parents brought me here when I was little?

LUCY. How old were you?

CLARA. Let's say three.

MARISELA. Or seven. Kids don't make decisions, they grow up where their parents take them.

LUCY. The parents should have thought about their kids. They are doing something wrong.

CLARA. They're just trying to give their kids a better life!

LUCY. But is stealing to get a better life, OK?

HELEN. What do you mean, stealing?

LUCY. My father says they come here and get free medical care, and get on welfare!

YADIRA. Illegal immigrants can't and don't get welfare!

LUCY. Don't they get to go to the ER? Don't we all pay for that?

MARISELA. But *they* pay taxes, too, Lucy.

HELEN. Calm down, Marisela. So how do we solve this?

CLARA. We forgive everyone and let them stay.

LUCY. Forgive everyone and let them stay?

GIRLS. Yes!

CLARA. Isn't forgiveness important?

LUCY. Of course. But so is Reckoning. We are talking about the law.

MARISELA. Jesus broke laws too.

LUCY. Are you saying we should have no laws?

MARISELA. No –

LUCY. We should just open the floodgates and say, don't worry about our laws, we will forgive you in the long run. And then watch the entire world move here?

CLARA. Of course not.

LUCY. We already have millions of illegals here. I'm from Las Vegas. We are being overrun. I have to go to a private school because otherwise, I'd be the minority.

HELEN. So what should we do about the people already living here?

LUCY. If they broke the law, I'm sorry, but they have to go back.

MARISELA. What if they have kids in their family that are citizens. What happens then? Ship out Mom and Dad...leave the kids all alone?

LUCY. We don't do that.

CLARA, MARISELA & YADIRA. Yes, "we" do.

LUCY. That's terrible. But maybe it's the right thing in the long run. Maybe its what's best for everyone. I mean how else will it all stop? Americans taking advantage of illegals. Illegals taking jobs that they shouldn't. It has to stop.

LUCY. Coming here is a choice. Choices have consequences. Breaking the law is breaking the law. We all have a responsibility to be the best person we can be!

MARISELA. That's exactly why people come here!

LUCY. No it's not. Because if it was, we wouldn't be fighting!!!!

    (Silence.)

I'm sorry. I'm not used to yelling.

HELEN. It's a very tough subject. Thank you for sharing your thoughts.

MARISELA. Yeah…I learned a lot.

LUCY. Please, don't take this personally. This is not about you. I love you girls. You're awesome.

CLARA. Thank you.

LUCY. I would be so lonely at this school if it wasn't for you.

YADIRA. College can be very lonely.

LUCY. This is why my father says never discuss politics with mixed company. We get too upset. Let's all go see a movie. My treat. OK?!!! Clara?

CLARA. OK.

LUCY. Wonderful. I'll drop off my computer at my room and be back for you all in ten minutes.

    *(**LUCY** exits.)*

MARISELA. Oh, God. Helen, did you have to go there?

HELEN. I thought it was a very brave conversation, on both sides.

YADIRA. It was really awkward.

HELEN. It was difficult but I also thought it was illuminating.

MARISELA. I thought it was offensive.

CLARA. Lucy is well-meaning. She's just very sheltered. She's not racist, she's just anti-immigrant – or anti-people-without-papers.

MARISELA. She's definitely anti-people-without-papers.

CLARA. She invited me to her Bible study.

MARISELA. Lucky you.

CLARA. Well, who else has reached out to us? Really tried to be our friend?

MARISELA. Lucy thinks we should be thrown out. How friendly is that?

CLARA. She's trying. It's so different here from her conservative private high school. She's a little lost.

MARISELA. So are we!

CLARA. I like Lucy. Lucy makes me feel like I'm a normal college kid, you know. I've never had a white friend before. It makes me feel like I belong.

YADIRA. Oh. *(Understands.)* She makes you feel like you're really American, right?

CLARA. Exactly, she's cool.

MARISELA. Okay, Lucy is nice. But, she's not cool.

YADIRA. Whatever you do, you can never tell Lucy the truth about our status!

CLARA. OK…OK.

MARISELA. No!

CLARA. I get it!

YADIRA. I hoped she might change her mind if we told her the truth…but I don't think she would.

MARISELA. I probably shouldn't spend too much time with her. I might get so mad and not be able to keep my mouth shut.

    (**LUCY** *re-enters.*)

LUCY. Alright, girlies. I have my car. Let's go!

CLARA. I need a break.

YADIRA. Okay. Let's go.

MARISELA. I'm not going.

LUCY. Oh please, Marisela. I said I was sorry. It will be fun. After the movie – let's go together to a mixer. Please?

MARISELA. I have plans. Off campus.

LUCY. Why go off campus...when we have everything we need right here?

    (**RAMIRO** *enters, in a Ranchero hat, tight wranglers, belt buckle and boots. He's ready to go dancing.* **MARISELA** *takes off her robe and she has a fabulous dress on too.*)

RAMIRO. Qui'ubo, M'ija! Ya llegó tu papacito!

MARISELA. Ramiro! Ramiro this is Yadira, Clara, and Lucy.

YADIRA. Mucho gusto.

CLARA. Hola.

LUCY. Oh boy. You don't go to school here; do you?

RAMIRO. Nah, I'm a mechanic at Tito's Auto Repair.

LUCY. You're not a guy. You are a man.

CLARA. Lucy!

RAMIRO. I'm twenty-three.

LUCY. I'm sorry.

RAMIRO. Güerita...all's cool.

MARISELA. And Ramiro, this is Helen.

RAMIRO. Hola, Helen.

HELEN. Hola, Ramiro. Nice to meet you.

MARISELA. Helen is the reporter I told you about.

RAMIRO. So you just sit there and listen to them talk all the time?

HELEN. As much as the girls let me.

RAMIRO. So you like dancing, Helen?

HELEN. I don't really go dancing. Often. Ever. Never.

LUCY. I dance to Christina Aguilera. Love her.

RAMIRO. Qué bueno, güey.

MARISELA. Hey Ramiro…shouldn't we be going?

RAMIRO. De volada, linda. Guess what's playing tonight? *(Sings a chorus of a Ranchera song.*)*

MARISELA. Yeah! Wanna come? Girls? Lucy?

LUCY. Me? Salsa dancing…

RAMIRO. It's not salsa. It's Ranchera, with maybe a little bit of Cumbia. Ándale amiguita. I'll look after you.

LUCY. Another time.

CLARA. But we promised Lucy we would go to the movies.

MARISELA. OK, Brownies, stay there and be square.

HELEN. Marisela…is it OK if I come with you?

(*Beat.*)

MARISELA. You want to come, Helen?

YADIRA & CLARA. Really?

LUCY. To that part of town?

MARISELA. To dance to Ranchera music?

HELEN. Yes. If that's OK?

RAMIRO. With us?

HELEN. I can follow you in my car.

MARISELA & RAMIRO. Great!

MARISELA. Wow. Órale, Helen! Should I do your eyes with my makeup?

HELEN. Another time…

RAMIRO. OK! If Helen wants to see awesome dancing… then she has to see you at the club. Helen! Vámonos.

CLARA. Marisela, you promised you would give me a ride to work early tomorrow morning.

MARISELA. I won't stay out late, I promise!

YADIRA. Take care of Helen!

HELEN. I'll be fine girls. See you tomorrow.

GIRLS. Shake it, Helen!

*(***HELEN, RAMIRO,*** and ***MARISELA*** *all exit.)*

YADIRA. Come on, we're gonna be late.

LUCY. Helen seems so…ladylike. I can't imagine her at a salsa club. Can you?

CLARA & YADIRA. It's RANCHERA!

Scene: The Club

(Ranchera music in a Latino club.[*] **MARISELA** and* **RAMIRO** *dance an amazing Cumbia. Which ends in a kiss.* **HELEN** *begins to leave.)*

MARISELA. Helen, this is the one place I feel totally like myself. The one place I don't have to hide.

HELEN. Your dancing was extraordinary.

MARISELA. Thank you. It means a lot to me you came tonight.

*(***MARISELA*** suddenly hugs ***HELEN***.)*

Are you OK with directions getting back? Do you need my help?

HELEN. I'll be fine. See you tomorrow. Be safe.

MARISELA. Always.

HELEN. This evening, our usual roles are reversed; Marisela is in charge. And I realize she has been navigating a completely different road map than me for a very long time. And yet we both hope to get to the same destination.

---

[*] A license to produce *Just Like Us* does not include a performance license for any third-party or copyrighted music. Licensees should create an original composition or use music in the public domain. For further information, please see the Music and Third-Party Materials Use Note on page iii.

Scene: Back at the Dorm

(The **GIRLS** *are pacing. Worried.* **HELEN** *is sitting or standing.)*

CLARA. She's late.

YADIRA. Where is she? What could have happened?

HELEN. She was fine last night in the parking lot of Fantasía.

CLARA. That was twelve hours ago! What if she got detained?

*(***MARISELA** *walks in with her heels in hand.)*

CLARA, YADIRA & HELEN. Marisela!

HELEN. Are you all right?

YADIRA. It's noon. Where have you been?

CLARA. Did you spend the night with Ramiro?

MARISELA. That's none of your business.

CLARA. You're hours late. You said you would take me to work. I'm going to be fired.

YADIRA. Marisela, what's your problem?

MARISELA. Wait until I tell you what happened? The truck broke down and I was stranded. And my phone died. It was terrible.

HELEN. I'm glad you are safe now.

YADIRA. Why do you have to go off campus to all those "Charro" clubs?

MARISELA. "Charro"? I did nothing wrong!

CLARA. Why can't you just stay here?

MARISELA. So I can "dance" hip-hop with a bunch of white rich boys? I can't blend in the way you do.

YADIRA. You don't want to blend in the way we do. That's the difference.

MARISELA. Oh, so now that's how you're going to be, Snow White?

YADIRA. Helen, did you hear what she called me?

It's the way you act! Marisela you do these crazy things and Clara and I always have to help you.

CLARA. Sí, and cover for you.

YADIRA. When we started college, nothing changed! You still create all this drama. The parties. Late nights. The boyfriends.

CLARA. So many boyfriends.

MARISELA. Ramiro is different.

YADIRA. I'm sick of it! I want you to move out!

CLARA & MARISELA. What?!

HELEN. Girls, maybe we should all breathe for a moment –

YADIRA. I can't live with you anymore! ¡Ya no más, Marisela!

MARISELA. Fine! Miss Priss. No quiero vivir contigo tampoco.

CLARA. ¡Muchachas!

HELEN. Girls.

MARISELA. Whatever, I'm going to drag my mattress over to Clara's room.

CLARA. And live with me?

HELEN. Oh dear.

YADIRA. See! Clara doesn't want to live with you either!

MARISELA. Clara! ¿Es verdad?

CLARA. Marisela, I really need quiet to study.

YADIRA. Me too. Clara can live with me. And you can live with Clara's roommate.

MARISELA. Oh yeah, then who gets Helen?

HELEN. Ladies, calm down.

MARISELA. Argh! ¡Me vuelves loca! I am out of here!

YADIRA. Good. I never want to talk to you again.

MARISELA. Fine!

(A loud knock at the door.)

CARLOS. Yadira, abre la puerta.

HELEN. Who's that?

YADIRA. *(Surprised.)* It's my stepdad.

CLARA. He sounds mad.

CARLOS. Abre la puerta, por favor.

HELEN. What's going on?

CLARA. Why is he here?

YADIRA. He's been calling

CARLOS. Es una emergencia, Yadira.

YADIRA. I'm coming, I'm coming.

*(**YADIRA** opens the door.)*

¿Carlos, que pasó?

CARLOS. ¿Por qué no contestas mis llamadas?

YADIRA. I've been busy studying. I turned off my cell.

CARLOS. Necesitas venir conmigo y ayudar con la casa, con los niños.

YADIRA. ¡No! ¿Dónde está mi Mamá?

CARLOS. La arrestaron.

YADIRA. Mami's arrested?

CARLOS. La cacharon usando los papeles de alguien más y la van a deportar.

(**GIRLS** *reaction.*)

Tienes que regresar a la casa. Vivir con nosotros ¡Ahora! ¡Necesitamos tu ayuda!

YADIRA. No. I won't live with you.

CARLOS. ¿Qué dices?

(**CARLOS** *takes a step forward. The* **GIRLS** *do, too.* **HELEN** *stands.* **CARLOS** *sees* **HELEN.**)

HELEN. I think you should leave.

CARLOS. ¿Quién es esta gringa?

HELEN. Soy Helen Thorpe.

MARISELA. Es una reportera.

CARLOS. Díle que no se meta en asuntos que no son suyos.

MARISELA. He says you should mind your own business.

HELEN. Tell him I'm going to call security.

MARISELA. ¡Dice que va a llamar a la policia!

CARLOS. ¿Tú sabes que tu mamá esta embarazada, no?

YADIRA. She's pregnant?

(**CARLOS** *leaves.*)

My Mom's going to jail for using somebody else's papers.

HELEN. Oh, Yadira.

YADIRA. And she's pregnant.

MARISELA. Oh, Yadira.

YADIRA. Our house doesn't function without my Mom. Carlos...demanded I come back and take care of everyone. And I should. I should...but...

CLARA. You can't drop out of college to take care of the kids.

MARISELA. All your life you worked for college. This is what your mom wants for you.

YADIRA. My stepfather is so mad. What should I do?

HELEN. Yadira, it's a very difficult situation. I'm here to observe and learn. I don't know that I have the right advice.

MARISELA. First, you have to get everyone in your family to raise five thousand dollars to get your mom out of jail.

YADIRA. Five thousand dollars!

MARISELA. And then your mom has to decide if she stays to face charges...or runs.

YADIRA. Maybe my mom should flee to Mexico. And have the baby there.

MARISELA. That means she can't come back.

CLARA. Oh, God. Oh, God.

HELEN. I'm so sorry, Yadira.

YADIRA. How could my mom be so –! A stolen identity!

MARISELA. Helen *(Beat.)* can your husband help? He must know people.

HELEN. John is the Mayor. He can't be involved.

YADIRA. Especially, with an illegal immigrant that commited a felony.

CLARA. Don't say that about your Mami.

YADIRA. I just want my mom to be OK. Even if I don't get to see her again.

> *(**MARISELA** hugs **YADIRA** as **YADIRA** sinks down to the floor stunned, without crying. **CLARA** sits by her and puts her hands around her shoulders. **HELEN** puts down her pad and lets her hand reach out to touch **YADIRA**'s hair.)*

Our stories seemed like they were going to have a happy ending, but this, is always hanging over us.

(**RAMIRO** *enters. He sees the scene.* **HELEN** *pulls back.)*

HELEN. Hi, Ramiro.

RAMIRO. Hola, Helen. Yadira. Clara. Hola, Guapa.

MARISELA. Hey, Ramiro.

(**MARISELA** *and* **RAMIRO** *kiss.)*

RAMIRO. Is Yadira OK?

MARISELA. No, but don't ask, OK?

How did you get in the dorm without calling me first?

RAMIRO. The security guard knows my cousin Ramón. I came over to find out if you want to go to a baby baptism today at Salón Ocampo?

MARISELA. Whose baby?

RAMIRO. I don't know! My primo has a friend that's friends with the parents...and he said we could go. There's a band and lots of food and drink.

CLARA. And babies. Always babies at a baptism.

YADIRA. You should go, Marisela, I'm OK.

MARISELA. *(Looks at* **RAMIRO**.*)* I'd love to Ramiro. Pero I'm going to stay here with Yadira and Clara.

RAMIRO. Bueno, Chiquita. *(Kisses* **MARISELA**.*)* I'll tell you all about it. *(He exits.)*

CLARA. Are you going to marry Ramiro? Do you love him?

MARISELA. Ay Clara.

HELEN. Clara agrees to move in. Marisela agrees, and moves out.

HELEN. Yadira's mother Alma sits in jail.

And Yadira wrestles with plans to protect her younger sister.

And I wrestle with what I know and so much more with what I don't.

And suddenly I know this is not a magazine article. These lives cannot be condensed to a couple of pages. This story is a book.

Scene: The Dorm

(**HELEN** *takes her seat in the dorm room.* **CLARA** *is studying.* **YADIRA** *is folding laundry.* **MARISELA** *comes in with blasting music.*[*])

MARISELA. Brownies, I have something big to tell you!

(**MARISELA** *dances like crazy.*)

CLARA. Hey! We're trying to study.

MARISELA. Hey Brownies! Be Brownies. Go Brownies! Oh, Hi Helen!

HELEN. Hi, Marisela.

MARISELA. Are you OK? You look worried.

HELEN. The Mayor got an emergency phone call last night. I have a lot on my mind.

CLARA. Is everything all right?

HELEN. No. It's sad and very complicated. But I don't want to talk about it.

(**YADIRA** *turns off the music.*)

MARISELA. Oye, it's times like this that we need music the most.

CLARA. We must be discreet!

YADIRA. I don't want the RA to come here and get us in trouble.

CLARA. Zulema is living with us.

---

[*] A license to produce *Just Like Us* does not include a performance license for any third-party or copyrighted music. Licensees should create an original composition or use music in the public domain. For further information, please see the Music and Third-Party Materials Use Note on page iii.

HELEN. Your thirteen year-old sister is living in the dorm?

YADIRA. Zulema can't live with my stepdad while my Mom is in prison. I'm taking care of her.

CLARA. Yadira got her last night. She's in the bathroom. Crying.

       (**ZULEMA** *enters.*)

MARISELA. Hi, Zulema! Your lips look great.

ZULEMA. *(Sniffling back her final tears.)* Thanks. Strawberry sparkle.

YADIRA. So what is your "big" news?

MARISELA. It might cheer everybody up. I just met with the head of Theta Theta Nu Charter. And she totally encouraged me to start a chapter here.

ZULEMA. What does that mean?

MARISELA. It means we start a new sorority. An all Latina Sorority.

CLARA. Really? Us?

YADIRA. Aren't we already like a sorority?

MARISELA. We are friends. But we don't have a charter. Organized clubs can make things happen: dances, fundraisers. We can raise money for a scholarship for a freshman next year.

ZULEMA. That sounds so cool.

MARISELA. If just five of us pledge, it could be, like, one hundred dollars apiece. But if all fifteen Latina girls at DU pledge, it could be thirty-three dollars.

YADIRA. I can't think of that. That's money I might need to give Zulema.

ZULEMA. I'm planning on getting a job.

YADIRA. Mami wants you to keep your grades up.

ZULEMA. I think you should do this sorority thing. It sounds fun.

CLARA. I do like the idea of an organized club. We could do something important.

(*Enter* **RAMIRO.**)

RAMIRO. ¡Hola, mi amor!

MARISELA. Hola, Ramiro.

(**RAMIRO** *and* **MARISELA** *kiss.*)

ZULEMA. I thought Fernando was your boyfriend.

MARISELA. Uyy! I broke up with Fernando a long time ago. This is Ramiro. Zulema is Yadira's little sister.

RAMIRO. Hola, hermanita. ¿Qué pasa? ¿Qué onda?

ZULEMA. (*Giggles.*) ¿Qué onda tú?

RAMIRO. Hello Helen.

HELEN. Hi, Ramiro.

RAMIRO. No lo van a creer, but I almost got killed last night!

MARISELA. ¡No! ¿en dónde?

RAMIRO. ¡Pues en Salón Ocampo! En el bautizo.

HELEN. Salón Ocampo? Oh no! That's right, you were there last night!

CLARA. Almost killed at a baptism party? ¿Cómo?

RAMIRO. This guy started shooting when the party was over!

HELEN. Did you see it?

YADIRA. But that's a family place. There's kids there.

MARISELA. Did he hit anybody?

RAMIRO. He hit these two policemen. One of them died. A nice police too – he spoke to me in Spanish when I got there. And get this, the guy with the gun was Mexicano. And if he's the guy I'm thinking of, he has no papers.

CLARA, YADIRA & ZULEMA. ¡Ay no!

MARISELA. No! Stop it! There's no way someone without papers would be so stupid and kill a cop. No seas exagerado.

RAMIRO. I'm not exaggerating! I heard the shots; I saw the guy running away.

HELEN. It's all over the news. You haven't heard?

YADIRA. We've been dealing with other things.

HELEN. John and I were notified last night. Now it's on every station. And the front page.

(**CLARA** *switches on the TV.*)

VOICE-OVER. "Officer Donnie Young was reported dead from three gunshot wounds – The suspect, Raúl Gómez García – escaped and a massive manhunt is underway."

YADIRA. This is bad news. Really bad news.

(**HELEN** *switches off the TV.*)

HELEN. Ramiro, you should tell the police what you saw.

(*Everyone suddenly looks at* **HELEN**.)

ZULEMA. Oh-oh.

RAMIRO. I forget she's listening all the time.

HELEN. Ramiro, you have to tell the police. We have to catch this guy.

RAMIRO. Helen, I can't.

HELEN. A police officer is dead!

RAMIRO. Helen...

HELEN. He had a wife and two young girls!

RAMIRO. You know, I can't walk into a police station.

HELEN. You are an eyewitness. You can help!

RAMIRO. Help? Oh sure, help! Everyone is fine with us fixing their cars, cleaning their houses and taking care of their babies...but then some punk does something stupid...

HELEN. Ramiro, this isn't about you.

RAMIRO. No, it's about you. And your husband. Don't you understand, Helen? If I get deported, that hurts my entire family.

MARISELA. What do you mean it's about Helen and the Mayor?

HELEN. Raúl Gómez García – the man they think killed the policeman, worked at the Cherry Cricket Restaurant.

YADIRA. That place belongs to your husband!

HELEN. This spring, Raúl used forged documents to get his job.

RAMIRO. Like we all do.

MARISELA. *(Beat.)* Oh. No. No. The Mayor hired an illegal immigrant who killed a cop!

HELEN. It's more complicated than that. John put all his restaurants in a blind trust three years ago when he became Mayor. He doesn't manage them at all.

MARISELA. So you and the Mayor aren't really involved.

HELEN. Technically no...and yet... *(She puts her face in her hands in a complex mixture of stress, guilt and sympathy.)*

    (Silence.)

ZULEMA. This is bad for Mami, isn't it?

YADIRA. Zulema, this is bad for every single one of us.

> *(Projections of images and headlines from the manhunt for Raúl Goméz García, in the U.S. and Mexico.*)*

---

*A license to produce *Just Like Us* does not include a license to publicly display any third-party or copyrighted images. Licensees must acquire rights for any copyrighted images or create their own.

Scene: Alma's Goodbye (The Bus Station)

HELEN. *(To the audience.)* I had tried so hard to be an observer. To report the story…and now suddenly, I am the story. Officer Donnie Young's murder changes everything for so many. For his widow and two daughters. For the police force. For the Mayor. For the city and the State. There is a massive national and international man hunt for the murderer. Talk shows and radio shows are inundated with fevered talk about immigration. New laws are enacted. And all of it affects the girls and their world. Yadira's mother Alma, who is out on bond, decides to not face trial and to take a bus to Mexico.

ALMA. *(While hugging* **ZULEMA**.*)* Cuida a tu hermana.

YADIRA. I'll look after Zulema, Mami.

ALMA. Prométeme que te vas a cuidar. Que vas a estudiar. Que no vas a hacer tonterías como yo hice.

YADIRA. I'll study. I'll be careful.

JOSEFA. Me voy. *(She pulls* **ZULEMA** *off her gently.)*

ZULEMA. No te vayas.

       (ALMA *begins to exit.)*

¡No te vayas!

HELEN. Why did your Mother decide to leave?

ZULEMA. Because she has to.

YADIRA. My Mom used a stolen identity and got that poor lady in trouble with Immigration. After the Donnie Young murder – They'll make an example out of her. They'll give her a long prison sentence before they deport her.

ZULEMA. She doesn't want to have the baby in prison.

HELEN. Will you be able to see her again?

YADIRA. No. I thought about just leaving with her. But my Mami says our town is poor, full of stray dogs, and no work. She says it's not where I belong.

HELEN. What about Zulema? She can go back and forth.

ZULEMA. By myself? My Spanish isn't so good. *(Beat.)* I just want my Mom to come back.

> *(Bus honks. The projection of the bus travels across the stage and vanishes.* **ZULEMA** *runs toward the bus and weeps.* **YADIRA,** *apart, watches or runs to her and consoles her.)*

Mami!

YADIRA. Helen, we agreed to let you follow us and ask all these very personal questions because it might help other kids like us. But my little sister isn't part of the deal.

HELEN. I understand. I'm sorry.

YADIRA. I'm responsible for Zulema now. She already needs a new winter coat.

HELEN. What are you going to do?

YADIRA. I'm looking for a second job.

HELEN. Yadira, your schoolwork!

YADIRA. I'll do it. And I'll get a better job. Look, I just bought my first fake Social Security card. *(Shows it to her.)* Since the shooting...employers want to see an actual card.

HELEN. Yadira, you saw what happened to your mom!

YADIRA. I'm not stealing anyone's identity. These numbers are made up.

HELEN. It's still forgery!

YADIRA. I don't want to do this, but I feel forced to.

HELEN. Yadira. I hate to see you using these black market documents. I hate to see you of all people acting like an…

YADIRA. Illegal? Like a criminal?

Is it morally wrong that I want to work to help my family?

HELEN. You could land in jail. And what would happen to Zulema then?

YADIRA. I have to worry about Zulema now.

HELEN. You are putting you, your employer, and possibly other workers in a precarious situation. There must be another way than fraud and forgery.

YADIRA. Helen, my Mom is gone. I have to earn money.

ZULEMA. We're not all killers, you know.

HELEN. Of course, I know!

YADIRA. Zulema, ya. Helen is just worried. Don't be a smart mouth. Let's go.

(**YADIRA** *exits.*)

HELEN. Yadira has never spoken to me with such directness before. She is growing up fast. She has to.

Scene: Demonstration on Campus

(Projection: Image of an auditorium at University of Denver. Pictures of police. Anti-immigrant posters.* **MIKE McGARRY** *is at the podium. The* **GIRLS** *and* **HELEN** *sit in the audience, with a* **LOCAL BUSINESS LADY.***)*

McGARRY. Everyone take a seat please. I want to thank the University of Denver for allowing us to have a panel here on campus. My name is Mike McGarry of the Colorado Alliance for Immigration Reform.

(YADIRA, CLARA, *and* **MARISELA** *take their seats as does* **HELEN.***)*

HELEN. Mike McGarry...political activist, rabble rouser, and anti-immigration crusader. Intense, loud, brash. Did I say loud already?

McGARRY. Now is the time for action. These undocumented people are flooding our schools, our hospitals, our jails... they're killing our police officers. If we are to survive, we must take away all incentives for coming here, and focus on deporting those that are already sucking our country dry. I suggest stationing law enforcement officials at every type of public transportation in the country to detain anybody who cannot prove their legal right to be here. I suggest taking away all job opportunities, all medical services, and stopping all children from getting any schooling.

(Clapping.)

LOCAL BUSINESS LADY. I am a local business owner and I'd like to make a statement.

---

* A license to produce *Just Like Us* does not include a license to publicly display any third-party or copyrighted images. Licensees must acquire rights for any copyrighted images or create their own.

McGARRY. Yes?

LOCAL BUSINESS LADY. If Colorado attacks these immigrants, then you will just drive businesses into neighboring states. This summer, crops rotted on Colorado fields because there weren't enough immigrants to pick them. Colorado needs immigrants for our farms, our factories, our ski resorts –

> (**GIRLS** *clap.*)

Without this cheap menial labor, consumer prices would skyrocket. Thank you!

McGARRY. Ma'am, cheap labor has a high price. A deadly price. I would like to bring to the stage Carol Vizzi.

CAROL VIZZI. This year my son, Justin, was killed in Thornton, Colorado by a reckless illegal alien. Justin was knocked from his motorcycle and while my child lay bleeding, that man just sped away. Six months later, the police arrested Roberto Martínez, an undocumented worker who had – already – been arrested for driving under the influence; driving with a revoked license; a hit and run, and careless driving resulting in death.

> (*Reactions to the long rap sheet.*)

With that arrest record, why did the government not protect us and have him deported? Why do we continue to look the other way when people are breaking our laws? Why was my son's painful death not prevented? I lost him forever...and for what?

> (**CAROL** *is overcome with emotion and escorted to a chair by* **MIKE McGARRY**.)

TANCREDO. Thank you, Carol for sharing your story with us.

I am Congressman Tom Tancredo.

TANCREDO. This is a tough issue. It touches a lot of emotions. Especially after losing one of Denver's finest due to our Mayor's shameful hiring policies.

(Boos for Hickenlooper.)

Regardless of how controversial it may be...we need to amend the U.S. Constitution to prevent American citizenship from being given to children who were born to parents without legal status, saying: "No more anchor babies!"

Liberals view immigration as a massive infusion of potential voters for the Democratic Party. Some in the Republican Party look at immigration, as a massive source of cheap labor. But to be called a sovereign nation, a nation has to be able to control its own borders. It is controlling your own destiny in a way, and we, ladies and gentlemen, we don't control our own borders. And every time we let an illegal stay, we are aiding and abetting the demise of our American culture.

Let's take it back and Send Them Back!!!

(**TANCREDO** *and the like-minded* **AUDIENCE MEMBERS** *exit chanting,* "SEND THEM BACK! SEND THEM BACK!")

HELEN. *(To the audience.)* A part of me really understands the appeal and perspective of some of Tom Tancredo's arguments. There is no doubt that he loves our country; and that he is trying to protect an America he holds near and dear to his heart. But at the same time Tancredo is railing about illegal immigration, he is also using undocumented workers to turn his basement into a high-tech getaway. How do we justify using this cheap labor for our farms, cleaning crews, and remodeled basements...and then still turn around and say these laborers are a nuisance and a threat?

Scene: A More Perfect Union

MARISELA. I'm sorry, but that was not cool.

HELEN. Girls are you all right?

MARISELA. I'm sorry, but I'm not all right.

CLARA. I know there are a lot of bad sentiments towards immigrants, and I feel sad for that woman who lost her son…but…this…is *hate.*

YADIRA. Humans everywhere kill, they drink, they drive – it's a human problem. It's a drunk driving problem. I don't think it's an immigration status problem.

MARISELA. Things are getting so scary. Ramiro's father was deported for driving without a seat belt.

YADIRA. Ever since the Donnie Young murder…everyone is on edge.

>   (**PROFESSOR LISA MARTÍNEZ** *enters the auditorium.)*

LISA. I'm glad you ladies took my suggestion and came to the panel and rally.

CLARA. Professor Martinez!

MARISELA. I'm not! It made me mad and sad and scared.

LISA. Ah, but isn't that democracy? The right of others to peacefully express things with which you might not agree?

MARISELA. This rally looked like democracy, but it didn't… feel like democracy.

LISA. Interesting. Why not?

YADIRA. Because everyone in that room has a say about the laws that affect our lives –

MARISELA. – Except us.

LISA. Why is that?

>   *(Beat.* **GIRLS** *look at each other. Confess.)*

MARISELA. Because, Professor Martínez, some of us have no papers.

LISA. *(Makes meaningful eye contact with* **HELEN**. *She gets it.)* Oh – I see.

YADIRA. Yeah, that changes everything. Right?

LISA. Not really. Where do you live?

GIRLS. Here.

LISA. Do you pay taxes?

GIRLS. Yes.

LISA. And if you had a chance, would you choose to become an American citizen?

GIRLS. Yes!

LISA. So...you comply with our societal rules...but you get few of our advantages. You pay taxes. But you have no voice. And how many people are out there in your situation?

HELEN. Like twelve million people.

MARTÍNEZ. So...can we have a huge group of people living, working, and dying in this country without giving them a political voice and still call ourselves the land of the free?

CLARA. *(Discovery.)* I don't think so.

YADIRA. No.

MARISELA. Wait. Are you saying we should get the vote?

LISA. Well, philosophically if the United States wants to be a real democracy, it has two choices: it can either spend massive resources detaining, processing, and deporting all undocumented people living here, or – it can offer a path of citizenship to all persons already living within our borders.

CLARA. But what about all those people talking about keeping – America AMERICAN?

MARTÍNEZ. True. What about that? What is it about the U.S.A. that is so unique? So American?

YADIRA. *(Light bulb.)* This country was built on certain unalienable rights!

CLARA. Life.

YADIRA. Liberty

YADIRA & CLARA. And the Pursuit of Happiness!!

MARISELA. That's it! I get it! I really get it! WE THE PEOPLE. WE *(Motions inclusively.)* THE...PEOPLE ...it has to include us, too. Because we are all already here.

YADIRA. But the laws...we have no power to help change the laws.

LISA. How did women finally get the right to vote? How did the Civil Rights Movement overturn Jim Crow laws? How do disenfranchised people in the U.S. let their voice be heard?

CLARA. We gather –

YADIRA. We organize –

MARISELA. We march!!!

LISA. And that ladies, is how the United States of America works to form a more perfect union.

(The **GIRLS** *and* **LISA MARTÍNEZ** *exit.)*

Scene: Marisela's Protest

HELEN. *(To the audience.)* Suddenly a small Latina sorority is helping to mobilize the largest ever May Day Rally for Immigration Rights in U.S. history.

> *(We see the picture of the one hundred thousand people at the Denver rally, dressed in white for peace.)*

It is breathtaking to look at that ocean of white. There are so many people, and from this capitol, you can see them all.

FEDERICO PEÑA. *(At the podium.)* I am here today to ask that we recognize the immigrant workers.

HELEN. Federico Peña, businessman, Former Cabinet Member for President Clinton and the first Latino Mayor in Denver's history.

FEDERICO. We should admire them for cleaning our buildings, building our homes, working our mines, digging our ditches, and yes, even fighting our wars! We should conduct a full moral gut check as we watch immigrant workers wither in our deserts, drown in our rivers, and die on our highways. And let me be clear, they are not here to commandeer airplanes to crash them into buildings.

We stand here today as one America. Together we have a powerful voice.

> **(MARISELA** *walks to the podium.)*

MARISELA. ¡Justicia para todos!

CROWD. JUSTICIA PARA TODOS.

MARISELA. ¡Nosotros somos América!

CROWD. NOSOTROS SOMOS AMÉRICA.

> *(Projected: Justice for all! We are America!)*

MARIESELA. ¡Hoy, este día, me recuerda al movimiento Chicano, al movimiento de derechos civiles, al movimiento para los trabajadores migratorios! ¡Hoy, este día, estamos pidiendo justicia y libertad, y queremos amnistía! ¡Es nuestra responsabilidad seguir con este movimiento, para decirle a nuestros representantes del Congreso que no vamos a irnos, y si nos hacen salir, vamos a regresar!

¡Vivan los trabajadores! Vivan los inmigrantes! ¡Viva Colorado!

(Translated on the screen: Today I am reminded of the Chicano movement, the civil rights movement, the migrant farm – worker movement! Today we are asking for justice and freedom and we want amnesty! It is everyone's responsibility to continue this movement, to tell our congressional representatives that we aren't going to leave, and if they make us leave, then we are going to come back!)

(Roar of the crowd.)

(Projection: The whole crowd of immigrants in white projected all over the screens.)*

*(***HELEN***,* ***CLARA*** *and* ***YADIRA*** *enter and congratulate* ***MARISELA***.)*

HELEN. Marisela! When we first met, I never imagined that one day I would see you standing next to Federico Peña on the steps of the Capitol building, addressing such a crowd.

MARISELA. Well, Helen, no need to imagine it 'cause I just did it!

---

* A license to produce *Just Like Us* does not include a license to publicly display any third-party or copyrighted images. Licensees must acquire rights for any copyrighted images or create their own.

*(The **GIRLS** hug **MARISELA**.)*

CLARA. You were great! ¡Lo hiciste tan bien! ¡Bravo, Marisela!

YADIRA. There's maybe a hundred thousand people here!

MARISELA. Oh, I know what I want to do after college. I want to go to law school! I want to be a civil rights lawyer!

*(**RAMIRO** enters.)*

RAMIRO. Marisela!

MARISELA. Ramiro. Did you see me…in front of all these people? Power to the People! ¡Increíble!

CLARA. Wasn't she great?!!

RAMIRO. No. I don't think so.

YADIRA. ¿Qué dices?

RAMIRO. Marisela, I think doing this was bad. This is going to get the wrong people mad. This is so…rebelde and cocky.

MARISELA. But we are people. We have rights!

RAMIRO. No we don't. This demonstration is going to scare a lot of people. People are going to get fired. The government is going to start more raids.

CLARA. Calm down, Ramiro.

RAMIRO. I can't calm down. Everyone here is so happy and feels so…victorious…but the fact is you just made things worse.

MARISELA. Peaceful assembly is one of the pillars of this country.

RAMIRO. This is real life! Why go to college? You still can't get a job legally afterwards.

MARISELA. I have to do something with my life.

RAMIRO. Then marry me.

MARISELA. What?

RAMIRO. I love you. Marry me. Let's start a family. Let's really move on with our lives.

MARISELA. Ramiro, I need to finish school.

RAMIRO. Why? For what?

MARISELA. For me. For you. We grew up in this country.

RAMIRO. We grew up, illegally, mi amor. We are nothing to these people.

MARISELA. *(Beat.)* Ramiro, I don't think we should get married.

RAMIRO. Marisela?

MARISELA. I think we should break up.

RAMIRO. Really?!! What!! Why?

MARISELA. I don't want to be scared anymore. Not like you!

RAMIRO. You think you are an activist, la gran activista. But the truth is, you'll never be more than a supermarket cashier.

MARISELA. No! You watch me. I'm changing the world.

RAMIRO. Dream on, Marisela! It's going to get a lot worse for all of us.

HELEN. *(To the audience.)* Ramiro is right. Things do get worse. Immigration raids and deportations increase exponentially. The effect is palpable. At the May Day rally the following year, turnout shrinks by ninety-five percent.

(Everyone exits.)

Scene: The Trial

HELEN.   The accused murderer Raúl Goméz García is caught in Mexico by Mexican Federales after his grandmother turns him in. Mexico changes its extradition laws for this case and he is brought to Denver for his arraignment and trial.

> *(Actor playing* **MARISELA** *with hair tied back in an orange jump suit enters, head down, shackled:* **MARISELA** *is* **RAÚL GÓMEZ GARCÍA**.*)*

Raúl Gómez García and Marisela Benavídez are both the same age. Both of them were born in the Mexican state of Durango and each followed the same immigrant's trajectory, moving first to California, and then to Colorado.

But it is Raúl Gómez García who dominates in the press, on the radio, on television.

> *(We see the damning headlines about Raúl Gómez García's terrible crime and eighty-year conviction.*)*

Is this the image most of us see of "illegal" immigrants? In this case, it is true and it is ugly. But is it fair? Is it representative of the millions of people who live and work in the shadows every day? I wonder how the discussion on immigration might deepen and become more nuanced if people like Marisela and Yadira got equal time on the news. But they don't. Girls like Marisela and Yadira lead quiet, unnoticed lives.

---

* A license to produce *Just Like Us* does not include a license to publicly display any third-party or copyrighted images. Licensees must acquire rights for any copyrighted images or create their own.

(**RAÚL GÓMEZ GARCÍA** *transforms back into* **MARISELA** *by taking off her orange jumpsuit on stage and becoming a young girl before our eyes.*)

Scene: Marisela and the Police

(**MARISELA** *is driving, listening to music. She's wearing her DU hoodie. She suddenly hears a siren. She sees police lights.*)

COP. *(On a loudspeaker.)* This is the Denver Police. Pull over.

MARISELA. Ay Dios. Por favor, no. No. No.

(**MARISELA** *gets so nervous that she steps out of the car. The* **COP** *starts walking towards her.*)

COP. Stop! *(Points his gun at her.)*

MARISELA. Oh God. Please don't shoot me.

COP. You don't ever step out of your car, you hear?

MARISELA. I'm sorry!

COP. Get back in the car!

(**MARISELA** *does.*)

License and registration...

MARISELA. I'm a senior at DU. Here is my student ID.

COP. I said: License and Registration.

(**MARISELA** *looks for it in her purse. She decides to hand over her fake Mexican ID.*)

MARISELA. This is my Mexican driver's license. I'm an international student.

(**COP** *looks at it. He looks at her.*)

COP. Stay here. Don't move.

(**COP** *exits to his vehicle.* **MARISELA** *nervously dials* **HELEN.**)

MARISELA. Please be home…Please be home…

HELEN. Hello?

MARISELA. Helen!

HELEN. Marisela?

MARISELA. Helen, I need you to write this down. I've been stopped by the police.

HELEN. Oh no.

MARISELA. He pointed his gun at me. I'm alone.

HELEN. Where are you?

MARISELA. I think he's calling me in. I think he knows my license is fake. I think this is it.

HELEN. Marisela – you should call a lawyer.

MARISELA. No. Just listen and take notes, OK? I need you to talk to my mom and dad. It's not safe for them to come find me.

HELEN. I promise to talk to your parents. But what about you?

MARISELA. *(Her voice cracks.)* I was going to graduate in six weeks.

(**COP** *re-enters.*)

He's coming back. I need someone to know what is happening. Please, don't hang up.

HELEN. I'm here, Marisela.

COP. Marisela Benavídez?

MARISELA. Yes, Officer.

COP. Do you know why I stopped you?

MARISELA. No, sir. I don't think I was speeding. I was wearing my seatbelt.

COP. Broken taillight.

MARISELA. *(Defeated.)* Ah. A broken taillight.

> *(Pause.)*

COP. How long have you had this license?

MARISELA. Since...I learned how to drive?

COP. It's the best one I've seen, yet. *(Pause. He hands back the license.)* Happy Graduation.

MARISELA. Thank you, officer. Thank you!

HELEN. *(From the phone.)* Thank you!

> (**COP** *exits.*)

MARISELA. Goodnight, Helen. Make sure you put him in your book.

HELEN. I will. Goodnight.

Scene: College Graduation

(Projections of graduation. *"Pomp And Circumstance" plays.*)*

HELEN. *(To the audience.)* A few weeks later, I go to the DU graduation. Fabián and Josefa are there.

And so is the boy who's loved Marisela since high school.

JULIO. I love you, Marisela!

MARISELA. *(She blows him a kiss.)* I love you too, Julio!

HELEN. I guess Julio finally got old enough to meet Marisela's standards.

MARISELA. Helen, you made it! We were worried!

HELEN. I wouldn't miss it.

MARISELA. Where are my parents?

HELEN. They're up there.

JOSEFA. ¡Hola mi'ja! I so proud of you.

FABIÁN. ¡Así es! ¡Hola, hija! ¡Qué orgullo!

(Everyone waves.)

YADIRA. Cynthia Poundstone is sitting next to my sister.

CYNTHIA. Howdy!

ZULEMA. A-jua!

(The music starts and the **GIRLS** *start to march.)*

---

*A license to produce *Just Like Us* does not include a performance license for any third-party or copyrighted recordings, or a license to publicly display any third-party or copyrighted images. Licensees must also acquire rights for any copyrighted images or create their own. For further information, please see the Music and Third-Party Materials Use Note on page iii.

CHANCELLOR VOICE-OVER. Graduates of the University of Denver. Congratulations and Godspeed.

*(All the hats go up in the air in celebration. Everyone rushes to say hi to the **GIRLS** and then moves upstage to set up the party.)*

*(**ZULEMA** approaches in a provocative outfit.)*

ZULEMA. Good job, Hermana!

YADIRA. Thanks, Zulema.

ZULEMA. Congratulations, girls! *(She moves away to help set up the party.)*

HELEN. Is your sister going to apply to college next year?

YADIRA. No. She's almost flunked out of high school. It's so strange that Zulema might not even apply to college. Because she was born a U.S. citizen, I thought she was going to have no obstacles. But all the moving around, my mom being gone –

I wasn't grown-up enough to help her.

POUNDSTONE. Your leaving college would not help anyone.

*(**JOSEFA** approaches **YADIRA**.)*

JOSEFA. Yadira?

YADIRA. Si Señora Benadidez?

JOSEFA. Your Mami would be so proud. Lo hiciste. Lo hiciste.

YADIRA. I did it. I really did it!

*(**YADIRA** hugs **JOSEFA**. **YADIRA** cries for the first time in the play. All the **GIRLS** are moved and do a group hug, they pull **POUNDSTONE** and **HELEN** in too.)*

POUNDSTONE. If I were to get hit by a bus tomorrow, of all the things I've done in my life, this would be the most important.

GIRLS CHEER. A la BIO – A LA BAO, A LA BIM BOM BA: BROWNIES! BROWNIES! RA-RA-RA!

(Music: big dance party.)*

(After the music, everyone claps. **MARISELA** *gathers everyone, her parents and the* **GIRLS** *and* **HELEN** *in a circle.)*

MARISELA. Everyone....Julio and I have some big news.

JULIO. Great news!

MARISELA. We're having a baby!!!

JULIO. Isn't that fantastic?

ZULEMA. That's so cool!

*(***HELEN** *and* **CYNTHIA** *look at each other. Everyone is happy except them.)*

JOSEFA. ¡Qué maravilla! ¡Voy a ser abuela! ¡Abuela!

FABIÁN. *(Starts a little theatening but end up hugging* **JULIO.***)* ¡Bienvenido a la familia, Julio!

CLARA. I love babies! Love them!

YADIRA. Julio is a good guy Marisela. I am happy for you.

JULIO. I want Marisela to take over the world!

MARISELA. I'm so excited for the future!

FABIÁN. Tequila para todos.

---

* A license to produce *Just Like Us* does not include a performance license for any third-party or copyrighted music. Licensees should create an original composition or use music in the public domain. For further information, please see the Music and Third-Party Materials Use Note on page iii.

GIRLS. But NOT Marisela!!!

> *(They leave to have a drink.* **MARISELA** *sees* **HELEN** *lagging behind, maybe writing in her notebook.)*

MARISELA. Helen –

HELEN. Well, the timing is good – you waited until you finished college.

MARISELA. Are you upset about the baby? Are you disappointed with me?

HELEN. I don't know. I'm struggling with this, Marisela. You excel in school, and speak at amazing rallies and charm deans and then you turn around and are happy about this?

MARISELA. Why is my pregnancy a bad thing?

HELEN. It's just you are so young!

MARISELA. I'm twenty-two.

HELEN. I know there is a big tension between your – your – American Dreams and your – Mexican ambitions. I just thought you really wanted to go to law school.

MARISELA. I do. *(Beat.)* Wait. You think excelling at school is American and being pregnant is Mexican?

HELEN. That's not what I said.

MARISELA. It's what you meant. So is doing well in calculus Mexican or American? What about dancing all night? Is falling in love Mexican or American, Helen?

HELEN. All I know is having a kid is difficult. Going to school is difficult. Look at how much your parents struggle! I don't want to give all those people rallying against you any more ammunition.

MARISELA. But they don't know me. I'm a DU graduate too!

HELEN. Exactly, they don't know you and appreciate you like I do.

MARISELA. But you are disappointed.

HELEN. I care about you. I'm worried.

MARISELA. Why? Because I'm not behaving like a real American? Are you the "real" American? Are you THE American woman Helen?

HELEN. I'm one of many, many different American women.

MARISELA. No! You think that being American is being like you! Face it, when people say American – lots of people, sometimes even me, automatically think of someone like you. Which is ironic, because you weren't even born here. You, Helen, are an immigrant just like me.

HELEN. You are being very unfair, Marisela. I never forget I'm an immigrant. I never forget where my parents came from.

MARISELA. Except you aren't just like me, are you? And that's the problem. You keep comparing my story to yours. And you get to decide what about me is foreign and Mexican, and what about me is not. And that's what you are going to tell people in your book, aren't you? That's your story!

HELEN. Marisela, this is your story!

MARISELA. Really? Then why am I not the one telling it!

HELEN. For five years, I have shadowed you and sat in the background and actively listened to you. Why? Because I thought the national discussion on immigration was leaving out a vital perspective. I wanted to capture all the complexity and complicity of your situation. My short article went from a couple of paragraphs...to a long narrative to a book.

MARISELA. And I'm grateful. But it's not me. It's your view of who I am. Please tell people in your book, that I have a voice too! And tell them that my voice is not yours. Tell them I have an accent, and I love my parents, and I worry for my friends. Tell them I dance Cumbia, and eat hamburgers. Tell them that I work hard everyday for what I got. And tell them that I feel that I am as real an American as one can be, except I'm missing an official piece of paper.

HELEN. I will, but Marisela, you have to understand –

MARISELA. No, you need to understand this. Being American isn't becoming just like you.

Being an American is having the opportunity to realize all the potential of being ME.

> (**HELEN** *sits down. She covers her face with her hands for a second.*)

Helen, are you OK? I'm sorry. I didn't mean to upset you. It's just...it's just.

HELEN. – I've misunderstood you. All this time, I thought being you was a struggle between two countries... two cultures, two "yous". And that one day you would end up fully on one side of that internal border. But that doesn't make sense, does it? There is no internal border. Everything you do is about everything you are.

MARISELA. Isn't that true for you too?

HELEN. Yes. It is. You are an elegant, colorful, complex woman.

MARISELA. *(Smiles.)* An American woman.

> (**MARISELA** *hugs* **HELEN** *and exits.*)

Scene: The Wedding

(**JOSEFA** *runs in with Marisela's baby. She hands him to* **HELEN**.)

JOSEFA. ¡Helen! ¡Qué bien que estás aquí. Ayúdame con el bebé.

HELEN. Ay Emilio. ¡Qué lindo eres!

JOSEFA. ¡Qué bien hablas español!

(*Music, we see* **MARISELA** *enter with a veil and her family and* **JULIO**.[*] *A mute wedding scene upstage.* **HELEN**, *still holding the baby, watches a little then addresses us while it's happening.*)

HELEN. My book ends here, but the story of the girls – the story of these young women – and their parents, and brothers and sisters, and husbands, boyfriends, and friends and neighbors,

(*Looks down at baby Emilio.*)

the stories of their children –

– the stories of millions and millions of other unique individuals living in the margins just like them, continues.

(**JULIO** *and* **MARISELA** *kiss. Everyone hugs.* **MARISELA** *approaches* **HELEN**.)

MARISELA. Hi, Helen. Thanks for minding Emilo.

HELEN. He's a beautiful boy, Marisela!

---

[*] A license to produce *Just Like Us* does not include a performance license for any third-party or copyrighted music. Licensees should create an original composition or use music in the public domain. For further information, please see the Music and Third-Party Materials Use Note on page iii.

(**MARISELA** *takes him from* **HELEN**.)

MARISELA. He's a handful.

HELEN. You are a great mom.

MARISELA. Thank you. I want him to have a better life than me.

HELEN. Baby Emilio is a citizen. And his mother is a college graduate –

MARISELA. – I haven't given up on law school –

HELEN. – All of that will help.

MARISELA. My baby is a citizen. My husband is a citizen. Pray I don't get deported.

(**MARISELA** *and her baby join the wedding party.* **FABIÁN**, **JOSEFA**, **CLARA**, **YADIRA**, **JULIO**.)

HELEN. There is no neat final chapter. Because in the end this is what immigration is: inherently messy. The question of how we as a people, deal with people already living on our land, is a very complicated one. The issue bleeds. And we are all implicated.

JULIO. Helen! We need a wedding picture. Could you take a photo of us?

HELEN. Say queso!

EVERYONE. Cheese!

(*Flash!* **HELEN** *takes a photo of the entire wedding. Many pictures of immigrants from all over the world fill the projections landscape.*[*])